Mills & Boon ~~~~ **to Blaze.**

Dear Reader,

Welcome to the SONS OF CHANCE series, where the men are hot and the women are happy! Travel with me down a winding dirt road to the Last Chance Ranch, dedicated to the proposition that we all need a last chance to find whatever we deserve, especially love (and great sex). As you sit on the wide front porch of the Last Chance and gaze at the magnificent Grand Teton in the early morning light, you'll notice a tall, broad-shouldered cowboy climbing into a dusty ranch truck. That would be Nick Chance, the middle son. He doesn't know it yet, but his world is about to be turned upside down. And a brown-eyed beauty from back east will try to help him put it together again.

Don't you adore a man in boots, snug jeans and a Stetson pulled low over his eyes? Trust me, you'll have a *really* good time at the Last Chance Ranch. It's great to be back in cowboy and Blaze® country again!

Happy trails,

Vicki

WANTED!

BY
VICKI LEWIS THOMPSON

All the characters in this book have no existence outside the imagination of
the author, and have no relation whatsoever to anyone bearing the same name
or names. They are not even distantly inspired by any individual known or
unknown to the author, and all the incidents are pure invention.

First published in Great Britain 2011
Harlequin Mills & Boon Limited,
Eton House, 18-24 Paradise Road, Richmond, Surrey TW9 1SR

© Vicki Lewis Thompson 2010

ISBN: 978 0 263 88056 4

14-0211

Harlequin Mills & Boon policy is to use papers that are natural, renewable
and recyclable products and made from wood grown in sustainable forests.
The logging and manufacturing processes conform to the legal environmental
regulations of the country of origin.

Printed and bound in Spain
by Litografia Rosés S.A., Barcelona

New York Times bestselling author **Vicki Lewis Thompson** has been writing books for a few (cough, cough) years now, and she has a Nora Roberts Lifetime Achievement Award from Romance Writers of America to prove it. Turns out that after all these years and all these books, the process is as exciting and challenging as ever. In other words, the 101st book is no easier to write than the first! And she wouldn't have it any other way. This is a great job and somebody has to do it. She feels lucky that she's been allowed to share her fantasy world with readers everywhere.

To Daniela Cardy, talented research assistant,
photographer, writer, and most important, friend.

Prologue

May 1, 1937

CHANCE MEN ARE LUCKY when it counts. Sitting at a smoky card table in the back room of a bar in Jackson, Wyoming, Archibald Chance muttered his father's favorite saying as he tossed his last dollar into the pot. His buddy Seth had thrown in the deed to a worthless ranch called the Double Zero, because that was the only thing of value he had left.

At the end of the game, Archie possessed that rundown piece of property plus enough to buy gas to get there. Seth was busted and would have to live on the pittance his sister Eleanor made as a seamstress until he found work or drank himself to death.

Archie couldn't let that happen to his friend. Besides, there was the matter of Eleanor. Archie had been sweet on her for months and he had a hunch she liked him a lot, too. He couldn't abandon her, either.

He threw an arm around Seth's drooping shoulders. "You and Eleanor come to the ranch and work for me.

I can't pay you, but you'll have a roof over your head. We'll make a go of that place."

Seth looked doubtful. "It'll be a leaky roof. The Double Zero's in terrible shape. Nobody's lived there for years."

"We'll fix it up. Come on, Seth. You're out of work and my carpentry isn't in demand these days. We might as well take a stab at ranching."

"Ranching?" Seth laughed. "We got no cows."

"Don't worry about the details. The way I look at it, this is our last chance. Hey, that's perfect! My name's Chance, so we'll rename it the Last Chance Ranch. What do you think?"

"I think you're crazy, but what the hell? I'll go, but I can't speak for Eleanor."

"She'll go." Archie decided his father's favorite saying might be true, after all.

"How can you be so sure?"

"'Cause I'm asking her to marry me."

1

NICK CHANCE WAS PISSED. There was no logical reason to fence this rocky section of the Last Chance Ranch. It would make a lousy pasture and was too far from the barn to work as a corral.

But big brother Jack had decreed that it should be fenced "just in case" they'd need it someday. There went Nick's day off. Jack had discovered that Nick had no vet duties today, either at home or at any of the other ranches in the valley, so he'd handed Nick a posthole digger.

Nick had been tempted to suggest where Jack might shove his posthole digger, but going off on Jack wouldn't solve anything. The guy was harder on himself than he was on anyone else. The rollover that had killed their dad last fall wasn't Jack's fault, but nobody could tell him different.

So Nicholas Chance, Doctor of Veterinary Medicine, was driving one of the battered ranch trucks instead of his primo medical rig, and he was digging postholes that didn't need digging. What the hell. He'd work on his tan. Climbing out of the truck, he took off his shirt and tossed it into the cab. Then he grabbed his worn leather gloves from the dashboard.

Before he lowered the tailgate and got serious about the project, he parked his butt on the fender and took a moment to appreciate the view of the Tetons. A raven gave him a flyby and what Nick interpreted as a caw of approval.

He couldn't stay mad in country like this. His gaze roamed over the soft gray-green of sage livened up with spring flowers, including two of his mom's favorites—pink wild geraniums and sunflowers. Rain had fallen the night before, swelling the creek that he could hear gurgling, although it was hidden by evergreens.

He caught a whiff of loamy earth and wet pine needles. The June sun was warm, but not warm enough to melt the snow still clinging to the jagged peaks. Nick never tired of looking at them.

A favorite memory surfaced, as it often did when he gazed at the mountains. Jack, leaning against the corral, had informed ten-year-old Nick and nine-year-old Gabe that the mountains were named by a French guy and Tetons was the French word for tits. Nick and Gabe had fallen over laughing, but Jack, a worldly fourteen, had predicted that someday they'd find the subject of tits fascinating instead of screamingly funny.

Nick smiled. As usual, Jack had been right, although Nick considered himself more of a leg man than a breast man. Gabe, on the other hand, liked his women generously endowed. Jack generally did, too, although since last fall he seemed to have lost all interest in anything frivolous, which apparently included dating.

Nick had plenty of interest in dating and didn't consider it the least bit frivolous. But he had no current girlfriend, and Jack's slave driver mentality didn't leave much time for developing a new relationship.

Nick sighed and levered himself away from the truck. Jack's mom had taken off when Jack was a toddler, so losing their dad had hit him extra hard. Nick and Gabe still had their mom. So did Jack, but despite all the love Sarah Chance had given him, he'd never forgotten he was her stepson.

The guy had issues, and Nick understood that, but things would have to change soon or Nick would be forced to take him on, even if Jack was officially in charge according to the terms of their dad's will. Jack might be top banana, but Nick, Gabe and their mother, Sarah, each owned a fourth interest in the ranch, which meant they had some leverage.

At least they'd all agreed not to sell the place despite the outrageous price the ranch would bring. With very little private land left near the Jackson region, the Last Chance was worth a fortune. But it was not for sale.

That had to be some comfort to the hands, who loved living and working on a privately owned spread. These days the Last Chance raised horses instead of cattle, but it was still a working ranch and that was a triumph in today's economy. Making ends meet could sometimes be a challenge.

Jack seemed to take that challenge a little too seriously, though. His idea of a workday had expanded until everyone was putting in twelve to fifteen hours. The hands were ready to mutiny and their foreman had dropped broad hints about quitting.

Gabe was the lucky one, Nick mused as he let down the tailgate and grabbed the posthole digger. Gabe's cutting-horse events gave him an excuse to leave for most of the summer. He was the best competitor of all of them, and by riding in those events he promoted the Last Chance horses and theoretically brought in buyers. He also didn't have to put up with Jack.

Pulling one of Jack's surveyor's stakes out of the ground, Nick tossed it in the back of the truck and jammed the posthole digger into the dirt.

By his tenth hole he'd dug up enough rocks to last him the rest of his life, and stacked them in a pile about three feet tall, his personal monument to stupidity. He was sweaty and bored. Like all the Chance men, he was perfectly capable of manual labor. But he'd spent years in school to become a large animal vet partly because he preferred a mental challenge to a physical one.

Planting the posthole digger in the ground, he took off his gloves and tucked them in his back pocket. Then he pulled a blue bandanna out of the other pocket, removed his straw cowboy hat and mopped his face. After replacing the bandanna and settling the sweat-stained hat on his head, he started counting the remaining surveyor's stakes to see how many holes he had left before he could be released from bondage.

That's when he saw her. She stood facing him, about twenty yards away on the dirt road he'd come in on. She slowly lowered her big-ass camera complete with telephoto lens, but he suspected she'd already taken at least one shot of him, if not more. He decided if she had the balls to take a picture of a perfect stranger without asking, he could give her the once-over without feeling like a male chauvinist pig.

She was on the tall side, at least five-eight. She'd dressed in fancy brown boots, a long tan skirt and a pale yellow, sleeveless blouse. Both the blouse and the skirt buttoned up the front. Apparently he was more sexually deprived than he'd realized because his first thought was *easy access*.

Technically her short, curly hair was brown, but that didn't really describe it. In the sun it seemed to be made up of a dozen shades ranging from milk chocolate to bronze. She was too far away for him to see the color of her eyes, but close enough for him to tell she was pretty, with high cheekbones, an aristocratic nose and full lips. Large gold hoops dangled from her earlobes.

She'd slung a brown leather backpack over one shoulder, and he expected her to put the camera and telephoto in it now that she'd been caught photographing the locals as if they were some form of exotic wildlife. But she surprised him. Curving her lips, she raised the camera again.

He couldn't resist. With a grin, he tightened his abs and flexed his biceps.

ALL HER LIFE Dominique Jeffries had been criticized for being too impulsive. But after a two-year stint as Herman's girlfriend, she'd learned to rein herself in. Now that she was no longer Herman's girlfriend, having been traded in for his boss's daughter, she wondered if she'd forgotten how to be impulsive.

At least she'd come this far. After being humiliated by her ex, she'd desperately needed to get away. She'd chosen the place she'd dreamed about all her life—the Wild West.

And yes, she'd considered the fact that she might find a wild cowboy here, too, someone who would soothe her damaged ego. Her trip to Wyoming was a test to see if the old Dominique was still in there, and whether she dared let her out to play.

This authentic cowboy would be a perfect way to discover if she still had what it took to be spontaneous. But not too spontaneous. She wouldn't do anything to jeopardize the portrait photography business she'd built in Indianapolis. Much as she hated to admit it, Herman had helped her become financially stable for the first time in her life, and having money in the bank felt good.

But she had another sort of good feeling in mind today, one that came from flirting with a hunky guy. Her newfound cowboy was already making her laugh with his muscle flexing routine. "Nice pose," she called out. "Care to show me the flip side?"

He turned, displaying buns to die for and back muscles like she hadn't seen in…well, in two years. Herman wasn't much for working out. She took a couple of shots, but she was here for more than the photography. A camera functioned as an excellent icebreaker.

Talk about overkill. Her shirtless cowboy was taking care of melting any ice that might be in the vicinity.

When she looked at him, she was surprised there was still snow on the mountains.

She couldn't believe she'd happened upon such a great specimen of rugged Western male on her first day. This guy was the anti-Herman. And that was really what she'd come here to find. After being a good girl for two years, which had gotten her…well…*dumped,* she longed to be a little bit wicked.

"Got what you needed?" he asked over his shoulder.

Not quite, but Rome wasn't built in a day. "Sure. Thanks."

He turned around. "I should be thanking you. You gave me a break from digging postholes."

"Glad to be of service." She unscrewed her lens from the camera and stowed everything carefully in her backpack before walking forward. "I'm here on vacation."

"No, really?"

She laughed. "I know. Hard to believe. I'm sure I look very Jackson Hole to you."

"Depends." His gaze lingered as he surveyed her outfit. "We get Hollywood types up here."

Being mistaken for a Hollywood type gave her a needed boost. Being ogled did, too. When she'd thought herself in love with Herman, she'd considered him frugal. Now she saw him as stingy, both with his money and his compliments.

This cowboy didn't seem like the stingy type. She loved the way he talked, slowly and deliberately, which she guessed came from living in the wide-open spaces.

His eyes, she discovered on closer inspection, were green.

"I'm not from Hollywood," she said. "I'm from… actually, never mind where I'm from. It doesn't matter. I'm on vacation from that place. No need to mention it."

"Where're you staying?"

She considered that a promising question, as if he might like to know how accessible she'd be while she was in the area. "Here."

"Ah. Overflow from the Bunk and Grub, I'll bet."

"That's right. Somebody ended up staying an extra week so Pam sent me down here."

"Happens all the time. I hope you're not too disappointed to find yourself on a ranch instead of a cozy B and B."

"Not at all. It's magnificent." *And so are you.* It was okay for him to ogle her, but she felt uncool ogling him. Yet she couldn't help it. His bare chest was a sight to behold—dusted with reddish-brown hair, muscled, and gleaming with sweat.

He nudged his hat back with his thumb. "Bet they put you in Roni's room."

"I'm not sure. Is she a NASCAR fan? There's lots of NASCAR stuff in there."

"She's a mechanic for one of the teams, only comes home for holidays."

Dominique hoped Roni wasn't his girlfriend. She hoped nobody was his girlfriend. "I'm glad her room is available." *Are you?* She peeked at his left hand, but lack of a ring meant little these days.

"First time in Wyoming?"

"Yes. I wanted to see something different."

"You mean like mountains and moose?" His green eyes sparkled with laughter.

"I suppose you think it's funny that I wanted to take your picture." She was close enough to catch his musky scent. She used to love sweaty sex. Herman had been an efficient lover, a competent lover, but he preferred air-conditioned bedrooms, so there hadn't been much sweat involved.

"Actually, I'm flattered. It's not often some good-looking woman points a camera at me for no good reason."

"I had a reason." She hadn't meant that to sound quite so husky and seductive. She cleared her throat. "What I meant was—"

"No, no, don't backtrack on me. I liked the implication of the first answer."

"Which was?"

"That you think I'm hot."

"Maybe." She found his swagger incredibly sexy.

His smile revealed even white teeth. "For the record, I think you're hot, too."

Now that was good to hear. With such white teeth, he must not chew tobacco. She'd thought about that as she'd fantasized a close encounter with a cowboy. A chaw of tobacco didn't figure into her fantasy. *Eeuuww.*

He stepped toward her, the first move he'd made in her direction. "So what are we going to do about our mutual hotness?"

Her breath caught. She'd started this interchange,

but he'd just taken charge and issued a challenge. He probably expected her to turn tail and run.

She hadn't come all the way to Wyoming to run away at the first sign of adventure. She was bound and determined to rediscover her impulsive side. Her heart pounding, she stood her ground. "I'm not sure. Any suggestions?"

He hooked his thumbs in the belt loops of his jeans so that his hands framed his crotch. "I can think of a way to handle it."

She could tell he still expected her to back down. Well, he was in for a surprise. Trying not to hyperventilate, she gazed into his green eyes. "So can I."

He stared at her. "You're not playing games, are you?"

"No." She swallowed and tried to breathe normally. "Are you?"

"I was a minute ago, but…damn, lady. Are you suggesting what I think you are?"

Adrenaline poured through her system. "Look, the last month has been hell. My steady boyfriend dumped me when his boss's daughter proposed. I scheduled this vacation to get away, to be in a completely different environment, and I…" The adrenaline began to fade, leaving her shaky. "The thing is, we don't have cowboys in Indianapolis."

He studied her in silence.

Her words seemed to hang between them in an embarrassing display of misplaced chutzpah. She began to squirm. "Forget I said any of that. I'll be going now." She turned.

"Don't leave." He reached for her hand.

She felt his touch all the way to her toes. No, cancel that. She felt his touch all the way to her womb. Hands so callused and strong could heal her. But only if he truly wanted this.

She turned back to him. "If you're feeling sorry for me, then—"

"No, I'm feeling sorry for the stupid bastard who put career advancement ahead of being with you."

Hearing that from a sexy cowboy was worth her plane ticket and lodging. "Thanks."

"Come on." He drew her toward the truck.

She resisted. "I don't need you to drive me back to the ranch house. I'll walk."

His grip tightened and his gaze locked with hers. "I wasn't planning to take you back."

2

NICK WAS A FIXER. Pop psychology said that was his role as the middle kid in a family of three boys, and maybe there was something to the theory. He'd been drawn to veterinary school partly because he saw it as an alternative to hard physical labor, but mainly because he loved healing injured creatures.

He'd been the boy who brought home the strays, the birds with broken wings, even a porcupine once, which had not been appreciated by his family. But that was what the Last Chance Ranch was all about, giving people and animals a second chance at life. His grandpa Archie would want it that way.

He wasn't sure what his grandpa would have said about this woman, but Nick saw her as injured, at least psychologically. Some jerk had done a number on her and left her to bleed. Nick wanted to help.

He was honest enough to admit that wasn't his only motivation. Helping her would be a lot more fun than bandaging a horse's leg or delivering a breech-birth calf.

Thank God he had an emergency condom tucked in the glove compartment.

Jack wouldn't be happy that Nick hadn't dug all the required postholes, but in days gone by Jack would have quickly abandoned the postholes for a chance like this. Just because Nick's big brother wasn't interested in the opposite sex these days didn't mean Nick couldn't indulge. Besides, this was an act of mercy.

And sweet mercy, she had incredible legs. He had to remind himself of his noble intentions as he helped her into the truck and she was forced to undo the bottom buttons of her skirt in order to make the climb. Thinking about those spectacular legs made his own journey to the driver's side more difficult. The zipper of his fly pressed uncomfortably against his ever-expanding interest in the hot woman sitting in the passenger seat.

"If we're not going back, where are we going?"

"I know a place." He'd grown up on the Last Chance, after all, and that meant he'd been a teenager here. Teenagers always knew a place.

"Pam said there's a sacred Native American site on the ranch. She talked about a huge rock that glitters in the sun. Are you going there?"

"No." Hanging his hat on the gun rack behind his head, he put the truck in gear and continued down the road until he found the dirt track that veered off to the left into the trees. "That site is all about finding solutions to problems." He glanced over at her. "Not to brag, but I have a solution for yours."

Her cheeks turned a becoming shade of pink. "I've interrupted your work. Will you get in trouble?"

"Maybe." He had to concentrate on his steering because the rutted road wasn't maintained, but the image of her flushed cheeks made him want to kiss her there... and everywhere else that turned pink when she was aroused. "I have a feeling you'll be worth it."

"Do you have a girlfriend?"

"Would you believe me if I said no?" The prospect of holding a naked woman in his arms was wrecking his driving skills. He'd hit a couple of deep ruts he ordinarily would have missed.

"I want to believe you. I'd feel horrible getting involved with someone else's sweetheart."

He bet she would after what that a-hole boyfriend had put her through. "Trust me, there's no one in my life right now. I don't cheat."

"I'm not asking because I expect anything to come of this."

He laughed, which helped release some of his tension. "You should expect something to come of this. Or some*one* to come of this. That's why I'm driving back into the trees, so we can have a little privacy. You could get loud."

"You think so, do you?"

"I've known it to happen." This was the most exciting damn thing that he'd ever done. He was shaking with anticipation. He didn't even know her name, and he liked it that way. He'd never had stranger sex.

Realistically, he'd probably find out who she was later on today. She was staying in the main house, so they'd be introduced at some point, maybe even at lunch. That could be fun, too, when she learned he was one of the owners. She wouldn't expect a Chance to be out digging postholes. Jack's insane work ethic was turning out okay for once.

Nick didn't kid himself that today would be the start of something big. She'd already told him she was a tourist who'd come to Wyoming to get over her crappy boyfriend back home. Once he'd helped her with that, she'd return to Indianapolis and continue with her life. In the meantime, his long dry spell was about to be over. Hot damn.

He reached the small clearing where he used to bring his dates back in high school, before he'd become sophisticated enough to rent a room. It was a great spot, drenched with hot memories. The sound of the creek was louder here, although it still wasn't visible.

Birdsong echoed through the trees, and wild roses bloomed, their dark pink petals startling against the lush ferns sprouting beneath the branches. Pine needles crunched under the truck's tires, enveloping them in a woodsy fragrance. The ground would still be damp after the rain, but all the ranch trucks carried a folded tarp in the back for emergencies. This qualified.

Cutting the engine, he turned to her. "Here we are."

"It's beautiful."

He looked into brown eyes that reminded him of a doe poised for flight. After six years of veterinary work and a lifetime of caring for frightened animals, he guessed that she was rethinking her decision to allow herself this moment.

"You're beautiful." He reached for her, cupping the

back of her head. Her glossy hair slid between his fingers as he leaned closer.

Her spicy scent was temptingly unfamiliar. He noticed a tiny mole near the corner of her mouth and the tangerine color of her lipstick.

She took a breath. "Don't you want to know my name?"

He caught a whiff of peppermint. "Does it matter?"

"No."

"That's what I thought." He was about to kiss a nameless woman he'd met twenty minutes ago. What a rush.

DOMINIQUE FIGURED SHE HAD about two seconds to call a halt. Once he kissed her, there would be no stopping. The air in the truck's cab was thick with lust.

Then her two seconds were up. His mouth found hers, and the storm hit. She'd never kissed a man she didn't know. If it was always this exciting, she'd have to do it more often.

Although technically he started the action, Dominique quickly became an equal partner, giving as good as she got. His kisses were supple, talented and sexy as hell. With a grateful sigh, she surrendered to his probing tongue and the heady feeling of passion fueled by mystery.

Gasping, he leaned his forehead against hers. "I love your mouth."

"I love your tongue."

With a moan, he resumed the assault with ravenous

kisses, but they were no more ravenous than hers. He kept his mouth on hers as he began unbuttoning her blouse. She didn't know how they would manage to have sex in the cab of his truck, but she'd let him worry about that. She reached for the waistband of his jeans.

He drew back, breathing hard. "This is nuts. We need to get out. We also need…" He popped open the glove box in the console and grabbed a small foil packet. "Wait right there. I'll come around and get you."

Before she could reply, he'd bolted from the truck. Dear God, she hadn't even *thought* about condoms. Not once. Maybe everyone was right, and left to her own devices, she'd head into a ditch.

But she'd lucked out again and found a guy who was more practical than she was. That was a very good thing, because she'd never been this aroused in her life. She was so hot she was panting. Her panties were drenched and her nipples ached. She wanted her clothes gone.

She heard him rummaging around in the back of the truck and then something soft hit the pine needles on her side of the vehicle.

Instead of sitting here stewing in her own juices, she could do something to move things along. In moments she'd pulled off both boots and tossed them on the floor of the cab. She'd finished unbuttoning her blouse when he opened the door.

"I'm ready," he said.

Judging from the fit of his jeans, he most certainly was. His boots, she noticed, were on the ground next to a tarp. She swallowed. "Me, too."

His hot gaze moved over her. "Your boyfriend is an

idiot." Tossing the condom packet to the canvas tarp, he circled her waist with his hands and lifted her down.

Her bare feet touched canvas, and then she was lost in the sensation of his palms sliding up her bare back, followed by him unfastening her bra. He undressed her with the practiced ease of a man who knew what he was about, and in seconds she stood before him wearing only her ivory lace panties. A breeze caressed her skin, but his smoldering gaze reheated every inch the breeze touched.

Cupping her breasts, he stroked his thumbs over her taut nipples. "To think I'd considered this a wasted day."

She clutched the solid warmth of his shoulders and closed her eyes, the better to savor the sensation of those calloused thumbs ramping up the tension.

His breath feathered her lips. "You are so delicious. Thank you for this unexpected gift." Then he settled in for another toe-curling kiss. She'd always thought "toe-curling" was only a quaint expression, but this cowboy literally made her toes lift off the canvas.

Impatient, she reached for his zipper.

"Mmm." His groan of approval vibrated against her mouth.

She shoved the jeans down over his hips, and as they dropped, he stepped out of them without breaking their kiss. She shivered in anticipation. And gratitude. Fate had sent her a cowboy with all the right moves.

When he hooked his thumbs inside the waistband of her panties and sent them sliding to the ground, she borrowed his strategy and stepped out of them. She'd wondered if she'd have the nerve to carry through, but here she was, naked in the forest with a ruggedly handsome man. And that man was kissing her in some very interesting places. Dominique Jeffries was back, baby!

Ah, she'd forgotten how much she loved foreplay. This cowboy seemed to love it, too. He moved slowly from her mouth to the sensitive spot behind her ear before making his way along the curve of her neck and across her shoulder. After kissing his way down the inside of her arm all the way to her wrist, he repeated the process on the other side.

Her collarbone got its share of attention, and the indentation at the base of her throat. By the time his moist caress reached the swell of her breast, she was a ball of fiery need, flushed and craving…everything.

And he gave it. After paying homage to her breasts, he moved slowly to her navel. When he circled it with his tongue, she felt an orgasmic tug that made her tremble.

On his knees now, he caressed her thighs. With his warm breath on her curls, he wrapped a supporting arm around her hips as he slid his other hand up, seeking… Finding.

She gasped as he pushed two fingers deep inside at the same moment his tongue made contact with her flash point. One stroke, one flick of his tongue, and she erupted. Crying out, she clutched his head, both to keep her balance and to hold him there…right *there*.

Then she lost her battle with gravity as he urged her down to the tarp. Vaguely she was aware of the rough canvas against her back and the cushion of pine needles underneath that perfumed the air she dragged into her lungs in great gulps. Somewhere nearby a creek splashed over smooth stones. But her main focus was this man, divesting himself of his last bit of clothing.

Dazed as she was by her recent climax, she still possessed enough brain cells to appreciate the wonder of her cowboy's package. If this was an example of Wyoming manhood, the state had much to be proud of.

As he moved over her and braced a hand on either side of her shoulders, he smiled. Then with one smooth thrust, he shoved home. "Welcome to Wyoming."

"My goodness." She reveled in the sensation of being filled to the brim, almost to overflowing.

"You okay?" he asked softly.

Her heartbeat thundered in her ears. "More than okay."

"That's what I like to hear."

She gazed up at him, anticipation sending tremors through her. If this connection felt so amazing, what would happen when he began to move? Every nerve ending in her body was on alert, waiting.

He drew slowly back, and the sweet friction intensified the climactic hum building inside her. Forward again, and she started losing her mind. Three strokes later she came, filling the clearing with her hoarse scream of joy.

But still he didn't stop. Instead he increased the rhythm and shifted his angle. "Again," he murmured. "Once more."

She was nothing if not obliging. That new angle was

finding all sorts of places where she hadn't known she had places. And she was dripping with sweat, glorious sweat.

"Good?" He was breathing heavily, but seemed in complete control.

"Oh, yes." She, on the other hand, had absolutely no control. He was driving this bus and she was merely a very ecstatic passenger.

As she tumbled into her third orgasm, he groaned and moved in tight. The steady pulse of his climax kept time with the waves of completion rolling through her. It was, without a doubt, the best sex of her life.

Sated and relaxed, she wondered dreamily if she should catch the first plane out of Jackson. This experience had surpassed her wildest hopes and dreams. Her vacation could only go downhill from here.

3

NICK HAD EXPECTED GOOD. Good would have done nicely to bind up her psychological wounds and scratch his temporary itch. Good would have made her fairly easy to forget when she left Wyoming. But just his luck, she'd turned out to be great.

Worse yet, he'd told her so as they laughingly searched for their clothes, both of them staggering a little from the effects of incredible sex.

"You were great, too." She smiled as she reached behind her back to fasten her bra.

He'd always adored watching a woman do that, and this woman was especially graceful at it. He had the urge to unhook her bra so she'd have to refasten it. But if he unhooked it, he'd want to touch her, and that would lead to more of what they'd recently shared. He wasn't sure where she stood on that issue.

"I can't tell you how this has improved my outlook," she said.

That statement had a ring of finality, of completion, as if one session had fixed her right up and she had no inclination for another round. Bummer. "How long are you here for?" he heard himself ask while pulling on his boots.

Damn, he'd probably tipped his hand with that dumb question. And an unnecessary question at that. He could find out when he returned to the house. Ordinarily his mom welcomed the Bunk and Grub overflow guests, but she was staying in town while Grandma Judy recovered from a hip replacement. Jack must have handled getting this woman settled, and would have all the details.

"Five nights," she said. "It was all the time I could spare from work."

"Which is?" He shouldn't have asked that, either. He was behaving like some lovesick fool desperate for information about the object of his affections. That was so wrong. They'd had terrific sex. Period. Sex wasn't everything. But…he'd never had any better than this.

She buttoned her blouse. "I guess there's no harm in saying. I own a photography studio. And before you get all impressed, let me assure you it's strictly a meat-and-potatoes operation. I specialize in family portraits, graduation photos and weddings. The basics."

"Nothing wrong with that." But unless he was reading her wrong, *she* thought there was something wrong with that. Her description of her studio invited him to dismiss it as pedestrian. "My mom treasures her wedding pictures," he said. "Especially since my dad passed last fall."

His mystery woman had leaned against the truck's front fender so she could pull on her boots. She paused in midmotion. "I'm so sorry. Was it sudden?"

"Yeah." And he wished to hell he hadn't brought up the subject. Way to put a damper on the proceedings. "Rollover."

"How tragic. How long were they married?"

"Almost thirty years. They got married after I was born. I guess it makes sense, considering the times. All that free love and flower power. But then my mom got pregnant again, and that must have tipped the scales toward matrimony." Sheesh. Maybe next he'd trot out the history of the Last Chance Ranch and regale her with that. He needed to shut up and take her back to... the road? Or the ranch house? Dilemma. He hadn't thought past the sex, but he'd better start thinking *tout de suite*.

A gentleman would take her back to the ranch house. He liked to think of himself as a gentleman, despite having just had sex with a woman out in the woods, a woman whose name he didn't know. But that had been gentlemanly, hadn't it? She'd needed something from him, and judging from her response, he'd provided it.

Turns out it was also what he'd needed, and would probably need again soon. That was the thing about good sex. It reminded you that sex was a lot of fun and should be enjoyed more often.

In fact, maybe there was a second condom...no, that was pushing it. This area was secluded, but not so secluded that someone might not show up. Like Jack, for instance, checking on his posthole digging. That thought prompted Nick to grab the tarp, fold it quickly and toss it in the back of the truck.

"You look worried all of a sudden." She finger-combed her short hair, which was still damp with sweat. "If it has to do with me tattling on you, then relax. That would be extremely ungrateful of me, to spill the beans and possibly get you fired."

"I appreciate that." He glanced down so she wouldn't see his smile. No matter what his transgressions, Jack was stuck with him. Although Jonathan Chance Sr. had specified in his will that Jonathan Chance Jr., aka Jack, was in charge, their dad had also dictated that his other two sons have jobs for as long as the Last Chance continued in operation.

Besides, Jack needed him. Nick was a damned good vet, and the horses bred at the Last Chance were valuable and required a vet on the premises. The Last Chance herd didn't take up all of Nick's time, so he had other clients in the Jackson Hole area, but his primary duty was to the LC horses. Even without the terms of the will to guide Jack's decisions, he wouldn't trust those animals to anyone else.

That wasn't to say Jack would let this little incident go if he found out. There was a time when he would have laughed about it, but he seemed to have misplaced his sense of humor. Nick would love to fix that problem, too, but so far all his attempts to get Jack to lighten up had failed. If his brother found out what had happened here, it could get awkward.

As if all this thinking about Jack had pulled him in Nick's direction, he heard the sound of hoofbeats. A few seconds later, Jack rode into the clearing on Bandit, a handsome black-and-white paint who'd been named for the masklike markings around his eyes. The ranch's top-earning stud, Bandit looked as if he could have belonged to a Shoshone chief.

Jack had some Native American in him on his mother's side, which explained his dark hair and eyes. Today he wore his don't-mess-with-me black Stetson, although it was covered with dust, as were Jack's jeans, his leather chaps and his long-sleeved shirt. He'd probably just finished a training session with one of the horses and was looking for something else to wrangle. His gaze swept over the scene, and his jaw tightened.

Nick did his best not to look guilty as hell. "Hey, there, Jack. What brings you out here?"

"Curiosity." His tone was even but his eyes narrowed as he focused on Nick. "I figured you'd be done with the postholes by lunchtime and it's nearly noon." Turning in the saddle, he touched two fingers to the brim of his hat. "Nice to see you again, Miss Jeffries."

Just like that, some of the mystery disappeared. Nick knew the last name of his previously anonymous lover. Soon enough he'd learn her first name, and he wasn't sure he wanted to know. What if it didn't fit his image? A woman who had stood naked and eager in the middle of a pine-scented clearing with the sun dappling her smooth skin deserved a really great first name.

He noted that Jack was behaving with polite formality by using her last name. No doubt Miss Manners would approve. Nick wondered what Miss Manners would say about using no name at all, particularly during the activity Nick and Miss Jeffries had engaged in. Nick didn't think there was a rule of etiquette to cover that situation.

The woman now partially identified beamed at Jack. "Nice to see you again, Mr. Chance. You'll have to blame me for the postholes not getting finished this morning. I was looking for Wyoming wildlife and your ranch hand was kind enough to escort me into the woods, where I'd have a better chance of finding it."

Nick almost choked as he swallowed a laugh. Damned if she hadn't told the truth. He was really starting to like this woman.

"I see." Jack folded his hands over the saddle horn and studied the scene. "In my experience, wildlife tends to come out at dawn and dusk."

Nick shrugged. "Usually, but it was worth a shot to accommodate a ranch guest."

"And it's a lovely spot," added Miss Jeffries.

"Yes ma'am, it is." Jack gave Nick another dirty look. When Nick and Gabe were in high school, they'd each claimed a make-out spot on the ranch. Jack had been their accomplice back then, supplying condoms from his personal stash and handing out sexual advice from his lofty, nonvirginal perch.

Nick wished the old Jack had shown up in the clearing instead of this new version. The old Jack would have smiled knowingly and headed back to the ranch house.

The new Jack glared at Nick with obvious disapproval. "I'd like those postholes dug today. The posts and wire should arrive this afternoon."

Nick met his gaze. "It'll get done."

"I surely do hope so. We've needed a fence out here for a long time."

Nick was willing to argue the point, but not at the moment.

Jack glanced up through the trees at the sun. The guy never wore a watch, never needed to. "It's late. Mary Lou's probably dishing up. You two better head back or you'll miss lunch."

"We'll do that."

"See you there." Jack touched the brim of his hat again. "Ma'am." Then he wheeled his horse around and cantered down the narrow road.

Nick wished she wasn't standing there watching Jack go with such apparent fascination. Jack might be bossy and abrupt these days, but women were still drawn to him. They always had been. For all Nick knew, Miss Jeffries might wish she'd thrown her loop at Jack Chance instead of some nameless cowboy wielding a posthole digger.

She turned to Nick. "What do you call that color horse?"

"Bandit's a paint. That's what we breed on this ranch." So maybe she'd been admiring the horse instead of the man.

"Show horses?"

"Can be. But we train and sell them as cutting horses, which means they—"

"I know what that is. I saw *City Slickers*." She ruffled her hair with her fingers again. "I think Mr. Chance had a pretty good idea what we've been up to."

"Probably."

"The way you talked back to him, I'm amazed you still have a job. Or maybe he didn't want to fire you in front of me. I'm perfectly willing to cover for you, but an employee needs to watch his attitude."

"Guess so."

"Yours was kind of belligerent, if you don't mind my saying."

Nick decided the game was over. "He can't fire me. I'm his brother."

Her eyes widened. "You're one of the Chance boys?"

"'Fraid I am."

"But…you were out here slaving away as if…"

"I know. It's a problem these days. Apparently Jack grieves by working around the clock, which is fine, except he insists the rest of us do the same. I'd rather not have a showdown with him, which wouldn't help morale, either."

She groaned. "And I've only made things worse between you during a tough time for your family. I'm so sorry."

"Hey." He rested his hands on her shoulders and looked into her eyes. "I'm a big boy and I make my own decisions. I don't for a second regret what we just shared. In fact, I was thinking that since you'll be here for five nights, we might—"

"Oh, no." She stepped back, out of range of his touch.

"What do you mean, *no?* Didn't you enjoy yourself? Scratch that. I know for a fact you enjoyed yourself. You couldn't fake that kind of reaction."

"But I thought you were one of the hired hands. Sure, I knew I might see you again while I'm here, but we'd pretend nothing happened so you wouldn't get fired for dallying with a guest."

He was picking up the drift of her comments, and he didn't like the implication. "So you bagged your cowboy, and now you're done?"

Her brow furrowed. "I told you I didn't expect anything to come of this."

"Yeah, but that doesn't mean it has to end with one brief moment in the woods! Hell, we'll be sleeping under the same roof!"

"Even more reason not to take this any further, especially with your brother monitoring everything that happens on the ranch. I don't want to be the cause of more friction between you two."

"Why don't you let me worry about that?" Nick was wondering if he could manufacture a necessary business trip for his dear brother, who was becoming an obstacle to all things happy.

"Let's just leave it alone. What we had today was perfect. I don't want to spoil it by turning it into some… some complicated maneuver."

Nick blew out a breath. "It doesn't have to be complicated. It could be very simple. I become your date for the time you're here and I inform my overbearing brother that it's none of his business what goes on between us."

"I don't think—"

"Look, I understand that you'll return to your life in Indianapolis in five days, and I'm cool with that."

"I'm not so sure I'd be. I don't trust myself not to get in over my head. I can't take that risk."

Nick gazed at her. "But you were willing to have outdoor sex with an anonymous cowboy."

"Yes. But now I intend to rein myself in."

"That's too bad. Plus, what else are you going to do while you're here? The skiing is lousy in June and I'm way more fun than a horseback ride or an all-day hike."

Her lips twitched, as if she wanted to smile but wouldn't quite let herself.

"Think about it, Miss Jeffries. In the meantime, let's hightail it to the ranch house before all the food's gone. I don't know about you, but I've worked up an appetite."

"Me, too, Mr. Chance." With a little grin, she walked toward the truck.

He had to clench his hands into fists to keep from grabbing her and kissing her until she melted against him the way she had earlier. He thought he'd done a damn good job of satisfying her, but maybe he hadn't pleased her all that much if she could turn her back on more of the same.

"The name's Nick," he called after her as she climbed into the cab.

"I like that," she said over her shoulder. "I'm Dominique."

Dominique. Great name for a very sexy lady. And he would get her into bed again or his name wasn't Nick Chance.

4

DOMINIQUE SPENT THE short ride back to the ranch house getting her bearings. When she'd first glimpsed a rugged cowboy working in a pasture, she'd thought Fate had sent her down that dirt road specifically to discover him. Everything had played out in fantasylike detail, until she'd learned the identity of her mystery lover.

An anonymous hired hand fit her image of wild and crazy behavior. She wouldn't say anything about the encounter and neither would he, for fear of getting canned. Very neat and tidy. Over and done with.

Had it gone that way, she could have rounded out the vacation by photographing the landscape, and flown home with a renewed sense of who she was. Her next guy wouldn't be as boring as Herman, or as disloyal.

But Fate hadn't been as kind as she'd thought. It had thrown a Chance man in her path, one who had the freedom to continue what they'd started, despite his brother's obvious disapproval. She dared not risk it. If the prospect of sex with him could make her forget about condoms, then he obviously appealed to a side of her she needed to control.

Besides, why mess with a good thing? She had her perfect memory to take home with her, and there was every possibility a second go-round wouldn't measure up. After two years with Herman, she had little confidence in her ability to improvise. What if they tried sex in a normal bed and Nick found her boring? She couldn't bear the thought.

In the midst of her inner debate, Nick reached over and took her hand. She had to admit that felt very good. She didn't know him at all, and yet she believed he was a nice guy. For sure he was an amazing lover, so amazing that he intimidated her more than a little.

"Look, you might have the wrong impression of me," she said. "Until today, I'd never had sex with someone I just met."

"Neither had I."

"Really? You seemed so…so cool about it."

He laughed. "Then I put on a good show. That was the wildest thing I've ever done in terms of sex. I kept wondering if you were part of a dream."

"I wondered the same about you. I actually pinched myself before I started taking your picture."

He squeezed her hand and released it so he could downshift. "Out of curiosity, what are your plans for those photos?"

"I suppose that depends on whether you'll grant me a release."

"Be happy to."

"Then I could…" She was brought up short by the

knowledge that this was the first picture she'd taken in ages where the subject wasn't a relative or a paying client. Her portfolio contained family portraits, wedding photos and high school yearbook shots. All her work prior to Herman's reign was tucked into the back of a closet, except for a few she'd framed and hung in her apartment.

"I know." He grinned. "You'll frame it and put it on your bedroom wall so you'll have something to remember me by."

His chutzpah made her laugh. "You have quite the high opinion of yourself, don't you?"

"If I do, it's your fault." He recaptured her hand. "You're the one who said you had to pinch yourself when you caught sight of me without my shirt."

She hadn't been teased much in two years with Herman, and she'd forgotten how fun it could be. "Maybe I was slightly mesmerized."

"Only slightly?"

"Okay, fully mesmerized. Which means other women might have the same reaction. I could make money off that shot. Maybe a gallery would be interested."

"Do you do that much? Display your photography in galleries?"

"Not anymore. I was going broke selling my work as fine art and borrowing money from my folks to keep afloat. My ex-boyfriend was right about one thing— weddings and portraits are a steadier income once you build up a reputation."

"Makes sense."

"Oh, it's very sensible." Herman's lectures on the

subject still echoed in her head. Her parents had been thrilled when he'd steered her in the direction of financial stability. Everybody had said Herman was so good for her, a practical guy to offset her tendency to ignore the mundane details of life.

His practical nature wasn't quite so attractive to her friends and family now that he'd applied it to his romantic life. But still they'd expressed fear that she'd go off the deep end without someone to counter her impulsive, artistic urges.

"Well, here we are." The truck's tires crunched on gravel as he pulled into the circular drive in front of a massive two-story log house. The center section was a good thirty feet wide, and the wings on either side were angled forward so that the house seemed to reach out in a welcoming gesture. A porch ran the length of the house, and rustic wooden rockers beckoned a visitor to sit and contemplate a view of meadows, wildflowers and snow-capped mountains.

Dominique had liked the white clapboard quaintness of the Bunk and Grub, the B and B where she'd originally thought she'd be staying. It sat on the outskirts of the little town of Shoshone, and she'd planned to explore the small village while she was here.

But she wasn't sorry Pam had moved her on down the road. Besides the obvious perk she'd just enjoyed in the woods, she'd be staying in this majestic ranch house. Pam had told her the ranch had been in the family for a long time. What a treat to grow up here.

"Was the house always this big?" she asked.

"Nope. The old house was trashed, so Grandpa Archie

built a two-story box with a sleeping loft upstairs. Then he added the right wing after my dad was born, and my dad added the left one after Jack was born. My mom was the one who insisted on the porches and a new kitchen and dining room."

"So the house has grown with the family. That's nice. I've never lived in a house built by the original owners."

Nick turned off the engine. "I can't think of doing it any other way. I'll probably build my own house when the time comes."

From the way he said it, she knew that time would be the day he decided to marry. She pictured the lucky woman and felt a pang of envy. Which was dumb, considering how little she knew about the guy. For sure he had a fabulous body and knew how to use it. But he could also have a thousand irritating habits that would drive a girl insane if she had to put up with him 24/7.

"So, before we go in, I have a suggestion." He glanced over at her. "How about me taking you into Shoshone for dinner tonight? They'll feed you here, of course, but I could show you the nightlife, such as it is."

She was sorely tempted. He looked mighty fine wearing his straw cowboy hat, faded jeans and a Western shirt with the sleeves rolled back. She knew the wonders hidden beneath that ensemble, and thinking about him naked made her mouth water.

But she'd had her impulsive moment, and she could tell this was a guy who would foster more of those. She still needed to exercise restraint even if Herman wasn't around, to keep from doing something foolish or jeopardizing the business she'd worked so hard to build.

"There's a funky bar called the Spirits and Spurs, and during the summer they have live music. The dance floor's small but adequate."

She could picture it—a cute little bar, some frothy glasses of beer and a tiny dance floor where they'd engage in that age-old foreplay ritual called dancing. She was a lousy dancer, but with a beer or two, she could fake it.

Regret tightened her chest as she gave him the only answer that made sense under the circumstances. "Nick, it wouldn't be fair for me to accept."

"Why?"

"Because I'm not going to have sex with you again."

His eyes became very green. "You're blushing, Dominique. I think you want to have sex with me again."

"That's not the point."

"It is the point. You want to and I want to. We're consenting adults who happen to be occupying the same place on the planet for the next five nights. I don't see the problem."

She did. Herman was a jerk, but he'd also stabilized her life. Maybe this man had been sent as a test to see if she'd revert to the person she had been, the one who dropped everything, including her financial obligations, when the next new experience appeared on the horizon.

She had to stay strong and focused. The trip had been excellent so far and she didn't need to go overboard in a way that would mess it up. Therefore she'd sleep alone tonight.

Facing Nick, she met his tempting gaze and said what had to be said. "I'm sorry. Thank you for a wonderful morning, but that has to be the end of it."

He threw up both hands in defeat. "I don't get it, but I've never begged a woman in my life and I'm not about to start now. Hold on a minute and I'll help you out."

"Not necessary." Dominique opened the door, which squeaked on its hinges. "But thanks."

He gave her an impatient glance. "I hope you're willing to walk into the dining room with me. Or would that compromise your principles?"

"Not at all." She climbed down from the truck and settled her backpack strap more firmly on her shoulder.

By the time she walked around to the other side, Nick was greeting two medium-size, mixed-breed dogs that had bounded over from the vicinity of the barn off to the right of the house. One was all black with longish curly hair and floppy ears. The short-haired one was tan-and-white, with a snub nose and pointed ears.

The dogs regarded her with curiosity, but Nick had a hand on each of their collars so they stayed by his side, glancing up at him with doggy smiles and wagging tails. Obviously they adored him.

"And who might these characters be?" Dominique asked.

"The tan one is Butch and the black one Sundance. Do you like dogs?"

"Yes, very much." Herman had talked her out of

adopting one, saying she couldn't afford the drain on both her time and financial resources.

"Go on over and say hello, boys." Nick released his hold and the dogs approached her with tails wagging. She crouched down and petted both at once. They sniffed her face and her hair, and Sundance gave her a little lick on the nose.

She had the ridiculous urge to gather the dogs in a hug. When she got home, she'd head for the nearest animal shelter and adopt herself one. "They're great," she said. "Where did they come from?"

"I found them wandering on the road about three years ago. Our golden retriever had died a couple of months before that, and a ranch needs a dog. Or two dogs. Besides, if I hadn't picked them up, they wouldn't have survived. My dad insisted on naming them after his favorite movie."

She heard the slight hitch in Nick's voice. Obviously he missed his dad a lot. "They're great names."

"Yeah." He cleared his throat. "Let's go get some lunch."

She'd just had sweaty sex in the woods and didn't feel quite ready to face public scrutiny. She gave the dogs a last scratch behind the ears and stood. "I need to stop by my room and freshen up before we eat."

His gaze traveled over her. "You look great to me."

She could say the same about him, but both of them bore the evidence of rolling naked on a canvas tarp in the woods. "Thanks, but if you want to go in together, I'll meet you back downstairs in five minutes." She ran up the porch steps and into the ranch house.

True to her word, she came out of her second-floor room five minutes later and found him waiting at the bottom of the curved staircase. His damp hair was combed and he'd put on a clean shirt.

As she reached the bottom step, a woman with fly-away gray hair barreled toward them from the hallway to their left.

"There you are!" The woman wore a red cowboy shirt with white piping, and jeans with enough stretch to accommodate her rounded figure. "Jack said you would be here for lunch, but I let everybody else go ahead because the food was getting cold."

"Forgive us, Mary Lou." Nick caught her around the waist. "But I'd rather have your cold food than anyone else's hot meal." He kissed her soundly on the cheek.

"Flattery will get you everywhere, Nicholas. Are you going to introduce me to our guest?"

"You bet." Nick swept a hand in Dominique's direction. "May I present Dominique Jeffries of Indianapolis. She's a famous photographer."

Dominique rushed to correct that misinformation. "No, I'm—"

"Dominique, this is Mary Lou Simms, the best cook in Wyoming."

Mary Lou smiled up at him. "Apparently I'm not that good or you wouldn't be late for lunch."

"It's my fault," Dominique said. "I got carried away by the photographic opportunities."

Nick pursed his lips and gazed up at the wagon wheel chandelier that graced the main room of the house.

"I love good pictures," Mary Lou said. "What have you taken so far?"

"Um, I took some pictures of Nick."

"Aha!" Mary Lou studied the man standing beside her. "Good choice. I assume you're into people instead of landscapes. I'm an Ansel Adams fan myself, but Annie Liebovitz has done some fine work. Her portrait of John Lennon and Yoko Ono is outstanding."

"I'm not in that class, Ms. Simms."

Mary Lou chuckled. "It's *Miss* Simms, and I'm proud of it. Never could see the point in marrying a man, although I've had my share of lovers. Couldn't have kids—lousy plumbing—so why tie myself down to a husband?"

"Sounds right to me." When Dominique had researched her trip to Wyoming she'd learned that it was the first state to give women the vote, and if Mary Lou was typical of the female population, Dominique could see why.

"Enough discussion," Mary Lou said. "My beef stew and corn bread aren't getting any better while we stand around yakking. I'll go make sure there's something left, but I'll ask you not to dawdle getting to the dining room." She bustled back down the hallway.

"I'll be there with bells on," Dominique called out after her.

Nick lowered his voice as the two of them followed in Mary Lou's wake. "Now that's the kind of response *I* was looking for."

"Let me put it this way. Mary Lou's beef stew and

corn bread is a whole lot safer option than spending an evening on the dance floor with you."

NICK'S MOTHER HAD designed the large dining room twenty years ago when the kitchen's plank table became too small to hold the family and all the ranch hands for the midday meal. Breakfast and dinner were served to the hands in the bunkhouse, while the family ate in a smaller, more intimate dining room, but Last Chance tradition dictated that everyone get together for lunch. Grandpa Archie had declared it was the best way to find out how the day was going for everyone.

The dining room was located at the far end of the left wing and had windows on three sides. Nick didn't often really look at it, but today, because of Dominique, he tried to see it as she would. He had to believe she'd like the arrangement.

Instead of one long trestle table, Sarah Chance had chosen four round wooden tables, each of which sat eight people. The ranch averaged a dozen employees, so the room was seldom filled, but it could be when horse buyers were in town.

Today about half the seats were empty. Nick chose a different table from the one Dominique picked, but positioned himself where he could watch her. If he'd been concerned about whether she'd feel comfortable walking into a roomful of men, he shouldn't have worried. She acted as if she sat down with ranch hands every day of the week.

Then he realized she'd have to be good at talking to strangers, both men and women. She took portraits for a living. Part of the photographer's skill lay in getting the subject to relax.

Nick wondered if she'd be inspired to take pictures of any of the other cowboys in the room. He didn't want her to do that, which was ungenerous on his part. She had the right to take as many pictures of cowboys as she wanted, and create a one-woman show with those photos in her bedroom back in Indianapolis if she liked.

He needed to accept her decision to have nothing more to do with him. But he couldn't help thinking that if Jack hadn't interrupted them, she might not be as jumpy about getting together. Nick could have eased her into the situation rather than have Jack be the black cloud raining on their parade.

Speaking of Jack, Nick didn't see him in the dining room. But Emmett Sterling, the fifty-something ranch foreman, happened to be sitting at the same table as Nick. Nick unfolded his cloth napkin, a dining room staple Mary Lou insisted on, and glanced at him. "Where's Jack?"

Emmett, whose salt-and-pepper hair, craggy features and solid build marked him as a man to be reckoned with, put down his spoon and picked up his coffee mug. "Ate fast and left. Said something about checking on Calamity Jane."

That was damned irritating news. "I checked her this morning. I give her at least another two or three days." He didn't appreciate Jack's behavior.

By announcing that he was going to see about the pregnant mare, Jack was implying Nick wasn't doing his job. Calamity Jane was Nick's responsibility and he was on top of it. She wasn't due for another week and had shown no signs of giving birth in the next twenty-four hours.

"Jack was just looking for an excuse to head for the barn," Emmett said. "He doesn't like hanging around during lunch."

"He used to." Nick glanced up to thank Mary Lou for putting a steaming bowl of stew in front of him.

"Are we talking about Jack?" Mary Lou plopped another basket of corn bread muffins on the table. "That boy isn't eating right and he acts like somebody shoved pinto beans up his nose."

"Or shoved them somewhere else," Emmett said with an evil grin. "Believe me, I've had the urge a time or two. What are we going to do about him, Nick?"

Nick glanced around at the expectant faces of the men at the table. "Damned if I know. Get him laid?" His response got the reaction he'd hoped for. Everybody had a good laugh, and most likely forgot their grievances against Jack, at least temporarily.

Emmett picked up a muffin and broke it in half. "Good luck with that. I think Jack's taken himself permanently off the market."

Nick thought so, too. His brother had been in town playing bedroom games with his girlfriend the day their father died. Although he had agreed to help their dad pick up a filly from a neighboring ranch, he'd begged off, claiming that a storm was coming and they should wait until the end of the week.

Their stubborn dad, who hadn't much liked Jack's girlfriend in the first place, had driven off to fetch the filly by himself. The storm had hit, making the roads slick.

Ironically, the filly, a brown-and-white paint named Bertha Mae, had survived the crash. Nick had doctored her minor wounds but nobody had ridden her since the accident.

Emmett leaned toward Nick. "Who's that good-looking woman you're keeping tabs on?"

And here Nick had thought he'd been subtle about it. "Her name's Dominique Jeffries. She's a photographer from Indianapolis. The Bunk and Grub ran out of room."

Emmett stroked his graying mustache. "Have you ever noticed that whenever the Bunk and Grub is overbooked, we always get the good-looking women over here? I can't remember ever getting a guy, or a couple, or a family with kids."

Nick had to agree that was true. "Maybe it's just easier to relocate a single person, and if you think about it, Pam doesn't get many single guys at the Bunk and Grub. I'll bet she has mostly couples and single women. If I were her, I'd move the singles to an alternate location before I'd move a couple, although I suppose that's some sort of discrimination."

"Your explanation is perfectly logical," Emmett said. "But my gut's telling me that Pam's trying to fix up those ladies with a cowpoke. Or fix up the cowboys with a tourist. I guess it could be either. Or both."

"I think it's pure coincidence." Nick took another bite of stew.

"Think what you want." Emmett helped himself

to more cornbread. "Oh, and by the way, that Jeffries woman is spending as much time checking you out as you've spent checking her out. I think you need to ask her to dinner."

Nick had known Emmett all his life, so there was no point in trying to maintain his manly rep with the guy. "I did ask her," he said. "She turned me down."

"And now she's looking at you as if you're the last piece of chocolate in the box. If I were you, I'd ask her again."

Nick shook his head. "I made my offer. The next move is strictly up to her." Swallowing another mouthful of stew, he decided to abandon the field. Let her come and find him if she'd changed her mind.

In the meantime, he would head down to the barn and have a word with Jack. The guy was getting on his last nerve.

5

DOMINIQUE DECIDED she was a hopeless case. Yes, she'd turned down Nick's offer, which was the sane thing to do. But she'd spent the lunch hour regretting her choice. She could probably handle another night with him. It wasn't as if she'd put a limit on how many sexual experiences she might have on this vacation.

She'd nearly made up her mind to go over and tell him she'd like to have dinner with him, after all, when he disappeared. She'd lost her chance, and trying to track him down was too obvious a move.

Excusing herself from the table, she climbed the curved staircase up to her room and grabbed one of the books she'd brought along. She could sit in one of the rockers on the front porch and read for a while. Nick might happen along while she was sitting out there.

On her way back down the stairs she paused to admire the room below. The focal point, on the wall opposite the front door, was a huge fireplace made of mammoth chunks of butterscotch-colored stone. Four brown leather armchairs plus one love seat were grouped in front of the fireplace, along with sturdy wooden end tables. Overhead was the expected wagon wheel chandelier complete with antique oil lamps wired for electricity.

No rugs covered the gleaming hardwood floor, but several hung on the walls. She was no expert, but the Native American designs looked handwoven and extremely valuable.

Logs were stacked on the hearth, and she could easily imagine sitting in this room before a blazing fire, curled up either with a book or a cowboy. Behind the large freestanding fireplace screen she glimpsed andirons in the shape of a horse's head. A thick slab of wood at least ten feet long formed the mantel, where framed family photos were displayed.

She decided to be nosy and examine them. As she came down the stairs, a good-looking older man walked in from the direction of the dining room. He carried his hat.

Pausing, he smiled at her. "Nick says you're a photographer."

"That's right." She held out her hand and introduced herself.

"I'm Emmett Sterling," the man said as he shook her hand.

"Do you work here?" Dominique didn't plan to make any more assumptions about who was hired help and who was family.

"I'm the foreman. Been here almost thirty years."

"Wow." She waved a hand at the mantel. "Then you could probably tell me about some of those pictures."

"I could tell you about all of them, probably bore you to tears with stories, but I have to get on down to the barn. We could have a situation brewing." He put on his hat and adjusted the brim.

"I understand. This is a working ranch."

Emmett laughed. "With *working* being the operative word these days."

"Nick mentioned that his brother Jack was pushing everybody pretty hard."

"That he is. Anyway, when you look at the pictures, you'll probably recognize Nick and Jack, since you've met them. The guy doing those fancy cutting-horse maneuvers is Gabe, the competitive one in the family. That trophy case in the far corner is a testament to his abilities."

"Wow." Dominique took note of the gleaming trophies. "He must be really good."

"He is, and his dad was right proud of him. Jack looks like his dad, so you should be able to pick out Jonathan Sr. The woman in the pictures with him is Sarah, his wife. Well, gotta go. Nice meeting you, ma'am." He touched two fingers to the brim of his hat and headed for the door.

"Same here. Thanks for the quick rundown on the family." Dominique turned toward the mantel just as the front door opened and Pam Mulholland, the owner of the Bunk and Grub, stepped inside. Dominique raised a hand in greeting and started to say something to her, but quickly realized Pam was so focused on Emmett that she hadn't noticed Dominique at all.

Emmett whipped off his hat in deference to Pam's

arrival, and Dominique was struck by how good they looked together. The B and B owner was probably in her late fifties, but she likely hadn't spent as much time outdoors as Emmett, so although his skin was more leathery, they might be about the same age.

Pam had colored her hair a pale blonde and wore it in a simple chin-length bob. She loved to cook, which showed in her dimpled cheeks and curvy body. Her warm smile transformed her from pleasant-looking to beautiful.

But she wasn't smiling now. She talked to Emmett in low, intimate tones, which made Dominique feel like an intruder. But if she walked away from them her boot heels would click on the hardwood floor and announce her as surely as if she'd spoken.

So she stayed where she was and pretended to study the back jacket of the book in her hand. She didn't mean to eavesdrop, but pieces of the conversation floated in her direction. She gathered that the discussion was once again about Jack and his overzealous work program.

"I can't take much more of it, Pam," Emmett said. "Life's too short."

"Promise me you won't do anything until I've talked with him," Pam said. "Please."

Dominique recognized that note of desperation in her voice; she was in love with Emmett. And Dominique had only to sneak a glance at the woman's face to confirm the fact.

She'd spent part of her childhood and a good chunk of her adult years behind the lens of a camera studying people's expressions. Catching that moment when someone revealed a deep emotion had fascinated her and propelled her into photography. As Pam gazed up at Emmett with wide eyes and slightly parted lips, she was telegraphing a total crush.

But she hadn't touched him. Dominique thought if they were having an affair, Pam would have at least laid a hand on the foreman's arm. He knew Dominique was standing there, but she had no idea.

"Okay, Pam," Emmett said softly. "I promise."

Dominique couldn't see his face very well, but she heard something special in his voice also. So what was keeping these two lovebirds apart? Although it was none of her business, she was dying to know.

After Emmett left, Pam glanced at Dominique in obvious surprise. "Oh, my goodness! I didn't realize you were standing there. How rude of me not to say hello when I first came in."

"You seemed preoccupied."

Pam sighed. "Emmett is threatening to leave the Last Chance, and that would be such a tragedy. He means a lot to this operation, and I think it means a lot to him."

And you mean a lot to each other. But Dominique held her tongue.

Pam seemed to give herself a mental shake before walking over with a smile. "Anyway, that's not your problem. How's your stay been so far?"

Dominique's cheeks warmed. That was a loaded question, although the woman had no reason to know that.

Pam looked alarmed. "If Jack's behavior is affecting

guests, then you don't have to stay. It's been a nice arrangement in the past, sending my overflow to the ranch, but I—"

"I'm having a great time." Dominique had never been very good at controlling her tendency to blush. She was pretty sure it was getting worse by the second.

"Then what's wrong? Something's turning your cheeks the color of a ripe tomato. Listen, if push comes to shove, you can have my room and I'll sleep in the parlor."

"Pam, I don't want to leave. Trust me, it's good here." She made a quick decision. She needed woman-to-woman advice, and Pam seemed like a sympathetic soul. "Maybe a little too good."

Pam's gray eyes lit up. "Oh? And how's that?"

"I've developed a bit of a crush on Nick."

Pam's dimples flashed. "Can't say I'm surprised. Does he have any idea?"

"In a way." Dominique didn't know Pam well enough to talk about what had happened in the clearing. "But here's the thing. I'll admit I came to Wyoming to get over somebody else. But I didn't come here to find another boyfriend. I've worked hard for two years to establish my photography studio in Indianapolis, and my roots are there. Crush or no crush, I plan to stay in Indiana."

"Oh." Pam hesitated. "Well, then I guess Nick isn't the right guy. That boy may not realize it, but he's primed and ready for Ms. Right. Worse yet, you're totally his type."

"In what way?"

"For one thing, you fit his physical profile." She laughed. "He confessed to me one night after a couple of beers that he's a leg man. You've noticed him, apparently, but I can guaran-damn-tee he's noticed you."

"I think so, yes."

"But you're his type in other ways, too. Nick has a sensitive, emotional side that would find happiness with someone who's artistic, who appreciates natural beauty the way he does. I was sort of hoping you two might hit it off, but if you're dead set on going back home…"

"I am." The conversation wasn't quite what Dominique had hoped for. She'd secretly wished Pam would encourage her to have a brief affair with Nick. Instead she was describing a man who would get attached, which wouldn't be good at all.

"Then I don't think it'd be a smart idea to get involved with him," Pam said.

"Right." Not sure where to go from here, Dominique took a calming breath. "So you know Nick pretty well, then?"

"Considering I've lived down the road for only five years, I guess I do. The Last Chance Ranch is my closest neighbor, and I've spent a fair amount of time here. All the Chance boys have their strong points, but I'll admit Nick's my favorite."

"I can understand why. He's great." And clearly Pam wanted to protect Nick from someone who had no intention of staying around. If Dominique had been wavering on whether to have a fling with Nick after all, she could kiss that idea goodbye.

NICK HADN'T PUNCHED JACK in years, but he might do it today. If so, he'd invite Jack to step outside the barn first. He didn't want to have a fistfight next to Calamity Jane's stall and risk upsetting the pregnant mare.

Butch and Sundance had followed him into the barn, and now they sat on the wooden floor glancing from one angry man to the other, their foreheads creased in doggy concern. Nick didn't want to fight in front of the dogs, either. But he had to say his piece and if that led to something physical, so be it.

"You're undermining my authority. The hands expect me to be in charge of any foaling that goes on around here. When you announce that you're going down to check on Calamity Jane, and I'm nowhere in the vicinity, they assume you're taking over my job."

Jack settled his dusty black hat lower over his eyes, which were the color of storm clouds. "Maybe I need to take over your job if you're going to be out in the woods screwing around with a guest when you're supposed to be working on postholes."

Nick jabbed a finger at him. "That's none of your business."

Butch whined nervously.

"The hell it isn't! She's a paying guest. Can you imagine the kind of trouble she could make for us if she chooses to? We could end up paying *her* to keep our reputation intact."

There was a certain amount of truth to that, which kept Nick from firing back a response. But he wasn't worried in Dominique's case. He hadn't known her long, but he'd known her intimately. She'd already made it clear that she wasn't a kiss-and-tell kind of woman.

"I'll take responsibility for any fallout," Nick said. He reached down and put a soothing hand on Butch's head. Butch was the more excitable of the two dogs.

"Easy for you to say, but ultimately I'm the one responsible for what happens to this ranch now that Dad's gone. And I intend to—"

"Work everyone to death?" Nick held Jack's gaze.

"That's what I pay 'em for, dammit! To work!" A muscle twitched in his jaw as he spun away.

"You're turning into a damned slave driver!"

Butch whined again.

"Yeah, well, here's a news flash. It's summer. This is when we have the best weather to train the horses. We always put in more hours in the summer."

"Not like this. Dad never—"

"I'm not Dad." Jack's eyes took on a dangerous gleam. "Are you challenging me, bro?"

Adrenaline rushed through Nick's system. Sex in the morning and a fistfight in the afternoon. It was turning into quite a day. "I do believe I am."

Jack braced his legs apart and flexed both hands. "Bring it on. Just know you're sticking up for a bunch of losers and whiners."

"Guess you can count me as one of them," Emmett said from the doorway of the barn. "I haven't had a day off in three months."

Beneath Nick's hand, Butch relaxed. Emmett had that effect on the dog.

Jack glanced in the foreman's direction. "Did you ask for one?"

"Yep. Couple of times. You said you couldn't spare me."

"You must have asked when things were crazy. That's how it is with ranch work. You take off when it's slow and stick with it when stuff piles up."

Emmett walked into the barn, his gait easy but his eyes like flint. "You know, Jack, I've been a part of this operation almost as long as you've been alive. I don't need a lecture on how a ranch works."

Jack faced him. "I take it you're not happy with the way I'm running things, either."

"I didn't say that. Matter of fact, I'm proud of the way you took hold of the reins, considering this situation was thrust on you sudden-like. We were all in shock and you stepped in and made sure the bills were paid and the routine was followed. That's admirable."

"But it's time to ease up," Nick said. "You're driving everyone too hard, including yourself."

Jack still wore that stubborn expression of his, the one that meant nothing was getting through to him. "You'd all be singing a different tune if revenues went down and the hands had to take pay cuts or get laid off."

Nick blew out a breath. "That's ridiculous. I've checked the books and we're nowhere close to that point. In fact, we're ahead of where we were last year."

He knew that didn't mean they were rolling in profits. The irony of the Last Chance was that their most valuable asset was the ground they were standing on. It had never been mortgaged, and nobody wanted to see that happen, but sometimes the ranch operations threatened to make that a real possibility.

"I'd think folks would be happy about our bottom line," Jack said, "not chewing my ass about the amount of work they have to do. But Emmett, if you need a day off so much, take one tomorrow."

"I do believe I will. You should take a day off once in a while yourself. It might sweeten your disposition some."

Jack made an impatient noise low in his throat. "Don't need one."

"Everybody needs time off, son."

"Not me. So are we done here? Because I have some things to take care of this afternoon."

Nick threw up his hands. "We don't seem to be getting anywhere, so I guess we're done. I have some postholes to finish up." He'd thought about refusing to dig the rest of them, but he'd promised, and he prided himself on keeping his word.

"What, you don't want the afternoon off?" Jack's taunting gaze dared him to wiggle out of the obligation.

"Nope. See you two later." He headed out of the barn, followed closely by Butch and Sundance. Good thing Emmett had shown up when he did, or Nick and his brother would have been trading punches by now. They might still end up that way eventually, but Emmett had defused the situation for a while.

"Hey, Nick," Jack called after him.

"Yeah?" He paused and turned back toward the barn.

"If you're going to poke around in the office, you

might as well make yourself useful. Sarah's been talking about going through that old trunk where Dad kept his sentimental junk, but she told me she can't bring herself to do it."

That Jack had insisted on using a first name for the woman who'd raised him from the age of four was another perfect example of the guy's stubborn nature. Nick's mother had asked Jack many times to call her Mom, but she might as well have made the request of a fence post.

"While she's in Shoshone taking care of her mom," Jack continued, "one of us needs to clean it out for her."

"I'll do it." Despite his irritation over being assigned another time-consuming chore, Nick hated to think what would happen if Jack went through that stuff. In his current mood, he'd probably toss most of it.

At least Nick had some time to do this task. His mother wouldn't be back for at least a couple of weeks, maybe longer. Grandma Judy's hip operation was a legitimate reason for her to stay in town, but privately Nick thought she'd been glad for an excuse to get away from the tension Jack was creating with his workaholic behavior.

The ranch truck Nick had used this morning was still parked in the circular gravel drive in front of the house. Now Pam's red Jeep was parked behind it. That made Nick remember Emmett's comment that Pam seemed to send only good-looking, single women over to the ranch.

Was Pam playing matchmaker? Was she here

checking on Dominique to see if she was attracted to any of the men around here? If that was Pam's game, she'd struck out this time.

Dominique wanted sex with no strings attached, and he was more than willing to accommodate her. Too bad she didn't seem to think it would work, now that she knew who he was. Figured. That's how his day had been going.

He should just get in his truck and drive back out to that rock-strewn pasture. Maybe he'd take Butch and Sundance with him. Digging holes might even be good for him right now, considering his frustration level.

Then he remembered that Emmett had said Dominique had spent her time during lunch sneaking glances at Nick when he wasn't looking. Maybe she'd changed her mind about having a five-day affair with him. If so, her nights here were limited and he didn't want to miss one.

He decided to make a detour into the house and see if he might run into her. He turned to the dogs. "You guys wait here. I'll be right back, and then we'll go for a ride, okay?"

Butch and Sundance sat beside the truck, looking expectant.

"Stay." Nick took the steps two at a time. If it turned out he and Dominique would be getting together tonight, after all, digging those postholes would be a lot more fun. Hell, he'd tackle that rocky pasture with his hands if it meant more great sex with Dominique when he was done.

6

DOMINIQUE WAS STANDING by the fireplace finishing up her conversation with Pam when Nick came through the door. Pam turned to greet him with a smile that told Dominique that for this childless woman, Nick was the son she'd never had.

The two women had exchanged a lot of information in a short time once they'd discovered a common bond—they'd each had the bad luck to hook up with a slimeball. Dominique told Pam all about Herman and Pam described finding her cheating husband with his secretary. That was six years ago, and Pam had taken him for every dime she could get.

Soon after that her parents had passed away, leaving her a large inheritance. Her only sibling had died in her twenties, so everything had gone to Pam, to her surprise. She hadn't spoken to her parents in years, ever since they'd disowned her sister for having a baby out of wedlock. Pam had assumed they'd donate their money to charity.

She'd sunk most of her newfound riches into the Bunk

and Grub and turned it into a successful B and B that was booked year-round. But guests came and went. The people at the Last Chance had become Pam's family, and everybody seemed happy with the arrangement.

Pam gazed at Nick with obvious affection. "Emmett was heading down to the barn. Did he locate you?"

"He did." Nick took off his hat as he came toward them. "I'm happy to say he's talked Jack into giving him a day off tomorrow. If Jack had refused, I hate to think how the conversation might have gone."

"But he didn't refuse, thank God," Pam said. "I made Emmett promise he wouldn't quit before I had a talk with Jack, but I don't know if that promise would have held in the heat of the moment."

"So we dodged a bullet today," Nick said.

"It seems we did. I wonder what Emmett will do with a whole day off?"

"Good question." Nick smiled. "Let's hope it's something he wouldn't ordinarily let himself do."

"Like a picnic." Pam's eyes grew dreamy. "I wonder if Emmett ever went on a real picnic."

"You should ask him." Dominique thought it would be fun to see those two get together while she was here.

Nick gave her a surprised glance, as if he hadn't expected her to come up with that. He probably didn't realize how quickly women could figure out the romantic lay of the land.

"I think you should, too," he said quickly, almost as if he wished he'd made the comment first. "Emmett might still be down at the barn with Jack. Drive over there, say I mentioned that he'd have tomorrow off, and invite him for a picnic. If you promise him your fried chicken and potato salad, he won't be able to resist."

Pam looked flustered. "He hasn't had a day off in ages. I'm sure he has a bunch of things he plans to do."

"Yeah, and none of them would give him the break he needs." Nick put his arm around Pam's shoulders and gave her a hug. "A picnic would be excellent, Pam. Do it."

"Okay, I'll see if I can catch him down at the barn." She hurried toward the front door, but then turned back. "I didn't get around to telling you, Dominique, but our Nick is a skilled veterinarian specializing in large animals. With the ranch's breeding program going full tilt, they couldn't do without him."

"I'll bet not." Add one more nail in the coffin of their potential fling, Dominique thought. The guy was an established professional firmly rooted in this place. He wasn't at all the devil-may-care cowboy she'd thought he was when he'd flexed his muscles for her out in the pasture.

"See you two later." Pam closed the door behind her.

Nick frowned. "That was weird. Why did she make that public service announcement about my job all of a sudden?"

"The operative question is why didn't you mention it to me before?"

"I didn't think it was important."

"It was. You led me to believe you were a cowhand

who spent his days roping dogies and putting up fence posts."

"Obviously I put up fence posts, but I haven't roped in ages. We train cutting horses and you don't use a rope for that maneuver."

She gazed at him and wished he didn't have all that sexiness going on with his short brown hair mussed from wearing a hat and those green bedroom eyes of his. Why couldn't he have a piece of carrot from lunch still stuck in his teeth? But no, he looked as yummy as ever, even with his shirt on. And he smelled so good.

If not for Pam's warnings, Dominique would be setting up their dinner date and checking her supply of condoms. "The truth is," she said, "that you're a guy who spent years in school to become a vet, one who only occasionally does that cowboy stuff."

"Hey, you're the one who wanted the cowboy fantasy this morning. I simply obliged."

"I have to give you props there. You obliged like a champ."

He drew closer. "And according to Emmett, you couldn't take your eyes off me at lunch. So come to dinner with me, Dominique."

"No can do." She stepped out of his reach, although it wasn't the easiest thing she'd ever done. She still wanted him with a fierceness that wouldn't go away.

"You're one maddening woman, you know that?"

"I'm doing this for your own good!"

"Oh, please."

"Seriously. Pam filled me in, and judging from what she told me before you arrived, you are beloved by most everyone, especially her. She wants the best for you, and she pretty much said you're not the sort of man to engage in a casual fling."

Nick stared at her. "So now *Pam* is the person who decides whether I have some fun this week? I like the woman a lot, but this is bogus."

"She loves you, Nick. She doesn't want you to get hurt."

"Good Lord. Why don't you ask me, the person involved, whether I can handle uncommitted sex? The answer is hell yes, I can. I'm a big boy. I know you'll go back to Indianapolis."

She was so tempted. God, was she tempted. But Pam had known this guy for five years, and if she thought an affair would turn into a disaster for Nick, then Dominique had no desire to take that chance. Pam probably knew him better than he knew himself.

But he might not appreciate hearing that. "Look at it this way. I like it here. As I told your cook, Mary Lou, I'm excited about the photographic possibilities and I'd like to come back."

"Even better. I'll have your bed waiting."

"That just won't work. Either one of us could be involved with someone else the next time, and it would all just be…awkward."

Nick slapped his hat against his thigh. "You're projecting problems into the future. Who knows what will happen? I'm in favor of enjoying the present, myself."

She smiled. "Now you're sounding like a soldier about to head off to war."

"Whatever works. Carpe diem and all that."

Dominique gazed at him with regret. "I'm sorry. I think it's a really bad idea."

"Well, you're the boss." He glanced into her eyes. "If you change your mind, I'll be out in that damned rocky pasture digging postholes. And I'll still have the tarp with me." Settling his hat on his head, he turned and walked away.

Once he was out the door, she unclenched her jaw. She had to physically restrain herself from calling him back. When she'd been talking with Pam everything had seemed so clear, but once Nick arrived and the phero-mones started flowing, she'd had trouble remembering why she shouldn't have sex with him again.

If she wouldn't be putting Pam out of her bedroom, she'd ask to return to the B and B. Or maybe she could sleep in the parlor. Dominique thought about that and finally dismissed it.

Much as she liked the quaintness of Pam's place, she preferred the majesty of the Last Chance. This house was masculine and bold, as were the men who lived here. Staying in this house stirred her sense of adventure.

Maybe she needed to channel her sexual frustration into photography. For the next five days she wasn't re-quired to take a single wedding shot or family por-trait. She enjoyed doing that, but it didn't feed her inner artist.

With a sense of excitement, she bounded up the stairs to get her backpack. She'd roam the ranch and see what sort of photo ops turned up. She would, however, avoid the rocky pasture where Nick was working. Another glimpse of his shirtless, sweaty body would wipe out every trace of her noble resolve.

AFTER DIGGING EVERY single damned posthole Jack had marked, Nick opened the passenger door so the dogs could jump into the cab. Then he drove back to the ranch house, showered and put on clean clothes. Dominique might not be interested in a night of dancing, but that didn't mean he had to sit home.

He was royally ticked at Pam for saying those things to Dominique, but he wasn't sure how to handle the situation. Pam had no right to butt in, and he'd have to set her straight about that, but he didn't want to hurt her, either. She meant well.

It might have been Pam's assumption that he wasn't capable of having no-strings sex that made him drive into Shoshone and park his truck in front of the Spirits and Spurs with the express intention of finding someone who wanted to take him home tonight. Or it might have been Jack's disapproval of what had happened out in the clearing this morning.

Or he might have wanted to show Dominique that if she chose not to spend the night with him, he could round up someone gorgeous who would jump at the opportunity. In any case, he had a wagonload of reasons why he was ready to raise some hell and find a willing woman to finish out the evening in style.

But three hours later he was back in the truck, heading down the road bound for the Last Chance, alone and disgustingly sober. He'd danced with every available woman in the place, which had left him little time for all the beer he'd planned to drink.

And as he'd made his way around the room, asking women to dance, he'd urged himself to settle on one of them as his partner for the night. At least two had seemed willing to accommodate him.

Sad to say, he couldn't work up any enthusiasm for the idea. Theoretically, it had sounded great to carouse the night away. In practice the effort seemed like a lot of work for very little payoff. None of those women could hold a candle to Dominique.

Which sucked on so many levels. He'd had one memorable experience with her, but he could not allow that to become his new benchmark. Outdoor sex with a nameless stranger was bound to be more exciting than anything he'd done before. He could remember it fondly, but he couldn't expect to repeat it or even come close to repeating it.

One comforting thought came to him as he parked the truck in his usual spot and walked into the house. She'd be in the same pickle the next time she thought about having sex with someone. No matter what venue she picked or who the guy was, it wouldn't be the same as spontaneous sex in the middle of a forest with someone she didn't know.

Nick would be damned if he'd let this obsession with Dominique rule his behavior. Next week, after she'd returned to her precious Indianapolis, he'd go back to the Spirits and Spurs and he wouldn't leave alone. Trying to do that tonight while Dominique was still here, while he could still remember the feel of her, the taste of her, the scent of her, had been too ambitious.

Downstairs was quiet, which wasn't surprising. Without his mom here to liven up the place, he and Jack became a couple of boring bachelors. Jack was probably already in his room, although Nick doubted his brother was asleep. He didn't sleep much these days.

Jack's room was on the second floor at the far end of the left wing, a room he'd chosen for himself when that wing was added. Gabe, who had always idolized Jack, had moved over to that wing, too, although Gabe wasn't home much anymore.

That had left Nick alone on the second floor of the right wing until the family took in Roni, a runaway teen. Now that Roni was off doing her NASCAR gig, Nick was by himself up there again, except for the occasional overflow guest from the Bunk and Grub. Which brought Nick right back to the subject of the current occupant of that room.

He was too keyed up to go to bed, especially when Dominique would be right down the hall. Might as well get started on that trunk of memorabilia in his dad's office—or what was rightly Jack's office now. Nick decided a beer would go well with that chore. After fetching a bottle of his favorite brew from the industrial-size refrigerator in the kitchen, he made for the office located on the first floor of the right wing.

The room was dark, but Nick knew the furniture placement by heart and walked without hesitation to his dad's desk. The old banker's lamp with the green glass shade was an antique his mom had found. His dad had loved that thing. Once Nick turned on the lamp, he found a coaster and set it on the battered old desk.

A new beer bottle ring might not matter, considering the condition of the wood, but Nick didn't feel he had the right to mar the finish with either a bottle or a boot heel. Only his dad had possessed that right. Even Jack was careful around it. In many ways the heavy wooden desk had represented their dad, and everyone treated it like a museum piece.

The wooden swivel chair behind the desk creaked in an achingly familiar way when Nick sat in it. Now that he was here and faced with the task, he wondered if he was up to it, after all. No telling what was in that trunk and what sort of memories, both happy and sad, those things would stir up. Happy memories might be the hardest to deal with.

Picking up his beer and nudging his Stetson back so he could see better, Nick swiveled the chair around. The leather trunk, about three feet wide and two feet tall, had been shoved up against the wall behind the desk for as long as Nick could remember. Nobody had been allowed to touch it except his dad, who had vowed that in his dotage he'd take everything out and make a big scrapbook, but in the meantime it was off-limits.

He'd never made it to his dotage.

After taking another fortifying swig, Nick set the bottle on the coaster, wiped his damp hands on his jeans and opened the trunk. As he'd expected, it was crammed helter-skelter with papers, photos, ticket stubs, horse racing programs and other bits of paper Nick would have to study to identify.

Obviously, this job would require more than one night, and probably more than one six-pack. But Nick was doing this for his mom, because she couldn't face it. He hoped *he'd* be able to face it.

As he started pulling things out, he ordered them in piles. Later he'd get boxes to put them in, but for now he'd use the floor.

A half hour into the process he took his empty beer bottle to the kitchen and brought back a fresh one. More than once he'd had to swallow some beer to wash away the lump in his throat. The trunk was full of heart squeezers, like the photo of the five of them grouped around a picnic table, or the ticket stub from a horse show on which his father had written "Took all three boys. Had great time."

Nick spent a moment studying the picture. Even though the five of them were together, Jack stood a little apart. He had always kept himself a bit separate, as if having a different mother than the other two boys meant he wasn't a full-fledged member of the family. How sad.

Putting the picture in a pile of others, Nick tackled more of the trunk's contents. His dad had saved correspondence from friends he'd made during his many years raising and training paints. Nick was eager to share those letters with his mom and brothers because they formed a picture of a man who'd been respected for both his talent with horses and his unwavering honesty.

As Nick delved further into the trunk, he came across a paper that didn't look like anything he'd found so far. It was a faded photocopy of an official-looking document dated, he noticed right away, on his birthday. Now there was a coincidence.

Curious, he began to read.

> To whom it may concern:
> I have on this day in Chicago, Illinois, given birth to a son, Nicholas Jonathan O'Leary. His father, Jonathan Chance, and I had a brief relationship nine months ago, but Jonathan does not know of this baby's existence, which is by my choice. However, should anything happen to me, I want Jonathan to be notified and Nicholas to be transported as soon as possible to the Last Chance Ranch in Shoshone, Wyoming, so that Jonathan may care for him there. My parents have no interest in the child and my sister is not of age.
> Sincerely,
> Nicole Elizabeth O'Leary

Nick stared at the piece of paper in his hand. Then he read it again. And again. No matter how many times he read it, and he soon lost count, the conclusion was the same. His entire life had been a lie.

7

DOMINIQUE WAS IN HER ROOM clicking through the photos on her digital camera when she heard Nick come in. At dinner she'd found out from the cook that he wouldn't be eating with them because he'd decided to go into town for a meal. Mary Lou had said that with a sniff of disapproval, as if she couldn't understand why anyone would choose a restaurant meal over one of hers.

Dominique had guessed that Nick had based his actions less on food and more on proving he could have a good time with or without Dominique's cooperation. The hands didn't eat up at the main house for dinner, so Dominique had been stuck with Jack in the small formal dining room until she'd begged Mary Lou to join them.

Fortunately, Mary Lou had been willing to fill in the gaps in conversation left by Jack, and the meal had gone well enough. Afterward he had excused himself and Dominique had hung out with Mary Lou in the kitchen, where she'd heard all about why Sarah, the lady of the house, was in town instead of at the ranch house. Mary

Lou had seemed glad for the female companionship with Sarah away.

But eventually the cook had toddled off to her quarters in the left wing, so she could watch her favorite TV shows, and Dominique had gone up to her room to look over the shots she'd taken during the afternoon. Or rather, she'd been trying to concentrate on the photos, but mostly she'd been imagining Nick two-stepping his way into another woman's bed.

She couldn't blame him for wanting to find someone more tractable than she'd been. She'd started his motor running and then abandoned him. For his own good, she reminded herself. In town he could look for someone who lived here, someone who might be a potential steady girlfriend.

Although she'd tried mightily to accept that scenario, she'd been pleased to hear him come in before ten. The lack of voices meant he was alone, although she doubted he'd bring someone back here, considering Jack's sour attitude. If Nick had found a likely candidate to replace her, he would have stayed in town.

She listened for his footsteps on the stairs and debated whether to come out of her room and ask if he wanted a nightcap. No, not a good plan unless she was prepared to alter her original decision. The reasons for not going to bed with him again still applied, so she'd be wise to stay in her room.

When he didn't come upstairs, she became curious. No one was around, so why would he linger down there? And he was definitely lingering. Finally she couldn't stand it. She crept barefoot out of her room and partway down the stairs.

From that vantage point she could see the light spilling out of a room that she'd identified earlier as an office. How ironic if Nick, who'd complained about Jack's overzealous work ethic, had come home early and was working on some ranch business.

She sat on the steps and contemplated her options. A sane person would retreat and go to bed. But at this hour she had trouble locating her saner side. The house was dark and silent except for the rustling of papers in the office and the occasional creak of a swivel chair.

What a bizarre situation, to be sitting in the dark listening to the movements of the man she'd had sex with twelve hours ago. She wanted to be with him, but his guardian angel in the form of his neighbor Pam had warned her off. Nick, however, would probably be thrilled if she showed up, especially if she proposed a repeat of their earlier experience.

When he walked out of the office carrying a beer bottle, she shrank back into the shadows, not wanting to be caught lurking there and essentially spying on him. But soon he returned carrying a bottle with condensation on the sides, and she realized he must have gone to the kitchen for a second beer.

That meant whatever he was working on didn't require total concentration or he wouldn't be doing it while sipping on a brew. Her presence wouldn't interrupt some important ranch business. The urge to wander down and see what he was doing grew stronger. She could use the excuse of showing him her recent photos.

Hugging her knees to her chest, she listened to him rustling papers. He sounded as if he might be sorting through something, maybe something private to do with his dad's death. Besides, what did she hope to accomplish by going down there?

Dominique didn't consider herself a tease, so if she set foot in that office, she should be prepared for the consequences. Nick would assume, whether she pretended it had to do with camera shots or not, that she'd changed her mind about having sex with him. Had she?

Her conscience was in a painful tug-of-war with her libido. With a sigh, she gave her conscience a hand and stood. She'd go back to her room, pull the covers over her head and forget about Nick Chance and his broad-shouldered, lean-hipped magnificence.

Feeling extremely virtuous, she started back up the stairs. That's when she heard Nick's gasp of surprise. She paused and listened intently for him to start rustling pages again. Nothing. Total silence.

She counted seconds in her head while keeping her ears tuned to whatever was happening in the office. He might have found something startling, but if he resumed his sorting, she'd go on up to bed.

But instead of rustling papers, Nick groaned softly as if in pain.

Dominique flew down the stairs and rushed through the doorway of the office. "Nick?"

He glanced up from the paper in his hand, and for a moment he didn't seem to recognize her.

She had no idea what was on that piece of paper, but judging from his stricken expression, it was bad.

"I…" She paused in confusion, unsure how to explain that she'd been eavesdropping on the stairs and had sensed something was very wrong. "I was passing by and I—"

"Dominique, please go to bed." His voice was hoarse, as if he could barely contain the emotion gripping him.

If she hadn't talked to Pam, if she hadn't learned enough about this man to know that he harbored all sorts of complicated feelings in that broad chest of his, she might have done exactly as he'd ordered. But now that she had a more complete picture, she wasn't about to leave him alone to deal with whatever shock he'd just experienced.

"I'm staying," she said. "I realize we don't know each other very well, but—"

"We don't know each other at all."

"That's not true. We shared something very basic this morning, and besides, there's no one around but me. Something is obviously wrong, and nobody should have to go through a bad moment by themselves if someone's on hand to offer…to offer…"

"Offer what?" He seemed dazed.

"What do you need?"

He scrubbed a hand over his face. Then he rose from the chair and laid his hat on the desk. "I don't think you want to hear what I need."

She swallowed. "Try me. If there's something I can do…"

"Oh, there is, but you don't think it's good for me." He sighed. "According to you and Pam, I shouldn't have temporary hot sex. That wouldn't be enough for a guy like me."

"I'm only going by what she said, and she's known you longer than I have."

His expression changed as anger sparked in his green eyes. "I doubt she knows the real me."

"Nick, what's wrong?"

He moved out from behind the barrier of the desk, his words rasping in the stillness. "Turns out I'm the bastard child of a casual affair."

"What…are you talking about?"

"That document I was reading when you came in lays it all out. My mother, who is *not* the person I've called my mother all these years, slept with my father and then moved on." He drew closer, stalking Dominique. "I'm the product of temporary lust, so why shouldn't I have those same urges? It's in my blood."

She struggled not to get swept away by the force of his anger-fueled desire. She didn't want either of them to do something they'd regret later. "You're upset, and I understand that."

"You asked what I need right now." His gaze was hot. "I need to be inside you. I need your warmth, your heat."

She began to tingle. "You're not thinking rationally, Nick. Give yourself time to cool down. Then you'll realize—"

"I'll realize that the only sanity I'll find right now is by thrusting deep inside you until I make you come." He cupped her face in both hands. "And make you come again, and again."

She closed her eyes against a wave of longing. "This is not the time."

"It's exactly the time." He brushed his lips over hers. "This morning you needed me. Now I need you."

Her heart squeezed at the vulnerability of that admission. "I don't want to make things worse for you."

"You won't." He ran his tongue over her upper lip. "Because you're real and you're honest. I desperately need honesty right now."

That she understood. She couldn't deny him the very thing she'd come here to find. "We don't have any…my purse is upstairs."

"This one's on me." He reached out and swung the office door closed before backing her up against it. "I left here tonight fully prepared to take somebody else to bed, but nobody could measure up to you." Then he kissed her, destroying any further protest.

Instead she aided and abetted, shimmying out of her slacks and underwear and working him out of his jeans and briefs. When at last she grasped the long hard length of his penis, she moaned with eagerness.

"Oh, yeah," he murmured against her mouth. "Touch me, Dominique. I want your hands on me."

There'd been no time for this before, but now she reveled in the chance to stroke and squeeze, rub and tantalize until his breath came in great gulps and he pulled back.

"Enough." Leaning down, he fished in the pocket of his jeans for the condom. Once he'd rolled it on, he cupped her bottom in his powerful hands. "Just hang on to my shoulders and wrap your beautiful long legs around my waist." He smiled for the first time since she'd come into the office. "Welcome to Wyoming." Then he lifted her up against the door and drove home.

The intense pleasure made her gasp in wonder.

He looked into her eyes. "It gets better. Hold on."

She gripped his shoulders as he began to move, his hips pistoning back and forth, up and in, as he made contact in all the right places and set off tiny explosions of delight. Each thrust pushed her back against the door and created a muffled thumping sound. The steady beat only added to the thrill. She began to pant as her climax drew near.

"That's it." His hot gaze captured hers. "Let go. There's more where that came from."

She groaned softly, reaching, reaching—and there it was, a release that showered her with wave upon wave of glorious sensations. She cried out and arched against him, only to discover he'd moved in closer with a hip grind that started the process all over again.

In a matter of seconds she was shuddering and gasping in his arms, her thighs slippery against his hips.

Sweat gathered in the hollow of his throat as he kept pumping. "One more, girl. One more."

"I don't know if I—"

"Sure you can. This time I'm coming with you." He picked up the pace, his fingers massaging her bottom as he plunged into her.

Amazingly, she felt the tightening begin again deep within her womb. She couldn't breathe, couldn't think. Couldn't imagine any reality other than this—the two of them locked together in a frenzied race toward a climax.

The door banged harder against its hinges, and as the moment of ecstasy hit with a vengeance, their cries of pleasure filled the small room.

Their harsh breathing rasped in the stillness that followed as they clung to each other. Gulping air, Dominique closed her eyes and leaned her head against the door. She'd had sex with this man only twice, and each time the act had been epic.

She knew he didn't mean to ruin her for anyone else, but she feared he was doing it all the same. Still, if she'd helped him through this wrenching moment in his life, the fallout for her might be worth it.

Nick let out a long, shuddering sigh. "That was… I don't have any words for what that was."

"Me, either." She opened her eyes and gazed at him. "Are you okay?"

"Better now, thanks to you." He drew back slowly, breaking the magical connection. "But I need to put you down before my arms fall off."

"Sure." She unwound her legs and hoped they'd hold her. "Don't let go yet."

"Don't worry. I won't let you fall." He steadied her as she slowly lowered her feet to the floor. "Are *you* okay?"

She smiled. "I can't remember the last time I've been this okay. But my legs are a little wobbly. I'll just lean here for a bit if you don't mind."

"Lean all you want. Just give me a minute." He turned away.

While he dispensed with the condom, she closed her eyes again and sagged against the solid door. She should probably look for her slacks and panties, but finding them wasn't a top priority.

Poor Nick. He'd suffered a terrible psychological upset tonight, but at least she'd been there to cushion the blow. She'd read somewhere that a shock caused some men to crave a sexual outlet. Nick apparently fell in that category.

Now that he'd released some of his pent-up emotion, maybe he'd be ready to talk about this startling information. She couldn't imagine what he must feel. His dad and stepmother must have had their reasons for perpetuating a lie, but learning the truth this way was so unfair to Nick.

When he turned back around, he was in the process of fastening his jeans. His gaze was decidedly calmer than it had been when she'd first walked into the office. "Thank you for being there for me. Seeing that document was…well, I sort of lost it for a while."

"I'm glad I was here." Crouching down, she picked up her slacks and panties. "I suppose now we should—"

"Take the party up to my room?"

She hesitated. Giving in to the moment was one thing, but planning to spend the rest of the night with him was a whole other matter. Pam's cautionary words came back to her. If Nick was likely to get attached, then he'd be even more likely now that they'd shared this pivotal moment in his life.

"I can see the wheels turning, Dominique. No, you don't have to worry that I'll fall for you because of what just happened. Matter of fact, I don't even know who I am anymore, so finding a steady girlfriend is the last thing on my mind. But lots of good sex would be a nice way to cope with—"

"Nick?" Jack's voice came from just outside the door. Then he pounded on it. "Open up."

Dominique looked at Nick, her eyebrows raised in question.

He shook his head and braced his hands on either side of her, keeping her where she was and using his weight to hold the door shut. "Lean back," he said softly.

She added her weight to his.

"Nick." Jack knocked again. "I know you're in there."

"So what if I am?" Nick reached down and flicked the lock closed.

"Don't you be locking me out! I demand to know what's going on."

"Go back to bed, Jack."

"I'm betting you're in there with Dominique. So help me, if you two are doing it on top of Dad's desk, there will be hell to pay."

A muscle worked in Nick's jaw. "You know what, Jack? There will be hell to pay, but it won't have a damned thing to do with Dad's desk. Or with Dominique, for that matter."

"Are you going to open this door or not?"

"I'm not. I do want to ask you something, and maybe it's better if we're on opposite sides of the door when I ask it. How long have you known that Sarah's not my mother?"

Dominique prayed that Jack would answer with words of shocked surprise, or maybe even denial.

Instead he muttered a few choice swear words. "You found something in that damned trunk, didn't you?"

"As a matter of fact, I did."

Jack swore some more. "Never occurred to me that Dad would be stupid enough to keep something incriminating in there."

Dominique's heart ached for Nick. Even his own brother had kept this life-changing secret from him.

Rage simmered in Nick's green eyes. "You know what, Jack? Dominique and I haven't done it on Dad's desk yet, but we just might. And as for you, my traitorous brother, you can kiss my ass."

8

NICK WASN'T ABOUT TO leave the office until he heard the sound of Jack's footsteps going back upstairs. Even then he didn't particularly want to go up to his room. Now that he knew Jack was in on the conspiracy, he needed some time away from his big brother.

Dominique wrapped her arms around him and he welcomed that. Right now she was the only person he felt he could trust. Good thing his mom—no, *Sarah*— wasn't around. He'd always claimed he'd inherited his sense of humor from her and his tendency to protect helpless, homeless creatures. Dear God, *he'd* been a homeless creature, brought here at such a young age that he had no memory of anything but this ranch.

He had so many questions, but he wasn't ready to face the people who could answer those questions—Sarah, Emmett… Emmett must have known. Probably Mary Lou, as well. Some of his dad's old friends who had come to the funeral must have been in on the secret.

Dominique rubbed his back and gazed up at him

with her warm brown eyes. "I'm so sorry, Nick. What a rotten way to find out something so important."

"Yeah." He leaned down and brushed his mouth against hers. "But you're here to ease the pain."

"Yes."

He noticed there was no hesitation in her answer that time. He drew back to study her. "Look, I don't want your pity. Your body, absolutely. Your pity, no way."

She grinned at him. "Hey, I'm just in it for the sex."

"Good. Me, too. I…" He paused to listen to measured footsteps on the stairs. "If I'm not mistaken, Jack is abandoning the field."

"Thank you for not confronting him while I was here."

"I'd like to take credit for being that sensitive, but I didn't want to see his face right now. In fact, now that the big bad wolf is no longer huffing and puffing at the door, I have a suggestion."

She slid her fingers up his chest and cupped his face in her hands. "After being caught by Jack twice in one day, I'd rather not take the risk of getting horizontal in your bedroom."

"Good, because we're setting a precedent for avoiding bedrooms, anyway. How do you feel about camping out?"

She looked doubtful. "I haven't camped out since I was in Girl Scouts in fourth grade. I wasn't much good at it back then. I'm not into creepy crawly things."

"I have a zippered tent that keeps everything out. Come on, Dominique. Consider it part of your Wyoming adventure. The camping supplies are down at the barn, so we can grab them and go."

"I'm barefoot."

He glanced down, noticing for the first time that she'd come into the office without shoes. Her toenails were painted the color of neon traffic cones, something he'd missed during their episode in the woods. He found those bright nails sexy, but then he found everything about Dominique sexy.

But she needed shoes, at least until he had her tucked into the tent. The concept of Dominique naked in a sleeping bag gave him an erection. He wondered if he was shamelessly using his personal crisis to get her to spend the night with him. Probably. But if Pam hadn't interfered, he'd have been able to work that on his own, so his conscience didn't prick him too much.

"Just run up to your room and grab some shoes and a jacket." He felt an urgency to get away, to escape from this house before Jack showed up again. "I'll wait for you down here."

"Are we going out to the clearing?"

"No."

"Then where?"

He'd wanted it to be a surprise, but she was still looking unsure of his plan, so he played his ace. "I want to show you our sacred Shoshone site." As he'd hoped, that tipped the balance in his favor.

"I'll go," she said immediately.

He wasn't suggesting it only to grab her interest. He felt a strong urge to go out there. For whatever reason, the large flat rock induced a feeling of peace, something he desperately needed right now. He hadn't been there since the day after his dad's funeral.

"Can I bring my camera?"

"It's dark, Dominique. And I'm not crazy about having you take flash pictures of me naked in the tent."

That made her laugh. "If I ever take pictures of you naked, I won't be using a flash. And it won't be in a tent. That sounds like a photographer's nightmare."

"So why the camera?"

"I have a feeling this place will be spectacular at dawn."

"It is, especially if there's no fog." Over the years, Nick had spent the occasional morning there watching the sun come up. Then his dad had died, changing everything. Partly due to Jack's relentless work schedule and partly because Nick had a tiny bit of that workaholic tendency himself, he hadn't felt free to wander out to the site the way he used to whenever he was troubled.

But he was way beyond troubled now. His dad's death had transformed the landscape, but this…this revelation rocked the foundation of his world. If he didn't go out to the site now, then he might as well give it up for good.

"All right," Dominique said. "Let's do it."

TWENTY MINUTES LATER Dominique sat in the passenger seat of the same ranch truck she'd ridden in that morning, as Nick drove slowly down a dirt road, headlights switched on high beam. He said that was to make sure they didn't run over any wild critters.

"Like what?" Dominique strained to see into the

darkness, but the headlights made everything else pitch-black, and there was no moon tonight.

"Whatever moves around at night. Coyotes, bobcats, skunks, raccoons, bears, snakes."

"Bears and snakes? Maybe you should take me back."

He laughed. "I'll protect you from the bears and snakes."

"So you say." Although Dominique had faith that Nick knew what he was doing out here, she was a city girl. Even during the few times she'd ventured into rural areas, they'd been a hell of a lot tamer than this landscape.

Nick rolled his window down. "Listen to that."

A distant howl drifted through the cool night air, followed by another.

A shiver of recognition traveled up her spine. She'd heard the sound on the Discovery Channel, but never in person. "Wolves?"

"Yep. It's a tricky balance in this area, because the ranchers don't want their livestock killed and the wild-life folks don't want the wolves to disappear."

"Have you had any problems with wolves on the Last Chance?"

"No. We lease about ten head of cattle for training our cutting horses every summer, and they bed down in the cow barn. The horses are in the barn closest to the house. We've made it work for us, but it's easier to do with our operation. Some cattle ranchers hate the idea of wolves."

"Wolves don't scare me," Dominique announced not

so convincingly. "I've seen documentaries about them, and they don't attack people. That's a myth."

"You're right, they don't. Most wild animals will give you a wide berth. We're far more dangerous to them than they are to us."

Dominique decided to roll down her window, too, and prove that she could be one with nature. By looking out the side window she could see more of the landscape. The road cut through a grassy field bordered by trees, mostly evergreen, judging by the scents wafting toward her.

Beyond the woods she could make out the jagged silhouette of the Tetons. Crickets chirped in the grass as they drove past, and a faint hoot of an owl told her that at least one perched in the trees, waiting to swoop down on its dinner.

The crickets reminded her of her grandmother's front porch swing in Wisconsin. Dominique used to sit there for hours as a kid listening to the sounds of the night. She drew in a deep breath and let it out in a sigh.

Nick glanced over at her before returning his attention to the road. "Was that a happy or a sad sigh?"

"It was my finally-starting-to-relax sigh."

Nick gave her another quick glance. "You know, I need to apologize for the tension around here. We've had a few of the Bunk and Grub's spillover guests since Dad died, but you're the first to stay here since warm weather hit and my brother turned into such a slave driver."

"It's okay. Pam warned me that Jack was on a tear, but she said you were really nice."

"I'm not feeling really nice at the moment. I'd like to

bash some heads, to be honest. It's good to know Pam didn't have anything to do with this massive cover-up. She's only lived here for five years, so I'm sure she bought the story Dad and Mo—" He broke off, then corrected himself. "The story Dad and Sarah cooked up."

Dominique picked her way carefully through what seemed to be an emotional minefield. "I haven't met Sarah, but Mary Lou thinks she hung the moon."

"Ha. I'm sure Mary Lou's in on this, too. She's been around at least as long as Emmett. You know, I can sort of understand not telling me when I was a little kid. I mean, Jack's mom, Diana, left, and that couldn't have been fun for Jack to live with. But at least his mom married our dad. As a kid, I wouldn't have understood why my mother didn't marry my dad—that I was…a mistake."

"Oh, Nick." The lights on the dash illuminated his rigid profile. "Nobody could get to know the person you are and call you a mistake. I told you—everybody loves you to death! I didn't meet your father and I haven't met your…your stepmother, but I can guarantee you gave them both joy." He'd given her joy, too, but she thought focusing on that would be unwise for both of them. She was a temporary solution to his angst, as he was a temporary solution to hers.

"I have to give Sarah credit. She treated all three of us exactly the same. She begged Jack to call her Mom, but Jack said Gabe and I were the only ones who had the right to use that word." Nick's laugh was hollow. "And all that time Jack knew I wasn't Sarah's kid, either."

"Jack must have willpower then," Dominique said. "I'm sure you two had fights. Heck, you almost had one today. At any time he could have used that information to hurt you."

"I guess."

She longed to put a comforting hand on his arm, but she wasn't sure if he'd welcome it. They had lust going between them, but that didn't make her a trusted friend.

Still, she hated seeing him in such pain. "Sarah obviously loves you as her son. Does it matter that she's not your biological mother?"

He gripped the steering wheel and stared out the windshield at the rutted dirt road. "Not if she and my dad had told me the truth once I was able to understand. I'm almost thirty years old and I know absolutely nothing about the mother who gave birth to me except her name. Worse yet, the one person who could have told me something about her is dead."

"I'm sorry. That must feel horrible." Dominique couldn't comprehend it. Her parents might not be perfect, but she had the birth certificate to prove they were definitely her parents. "Didn't you have to produce a birth certificate at some point in your life? I'm surprised you didn't find out that way."

"Looking back, I should have been suspicious. They never let me have my birth certificate. Dad claimed I'd lose it, so he or Mom, I mean Sarah, would go with me whenever I had to produce it. They must have clued people in ahead of time that the names on the certificate would be different from what anyone expected."

"That's amazing. They never intended to tell you, did they?"

"Doesn't look like it." He blew out a breath. "You know what? I'm not sure my last name is Chance. I could be Nick O'Leary."

"Probably not. I'm sure they fixed that legally right away."

"Yeah, I suppose. Otherwise things would have been even more weird." He slammed the flat of his hand against the steering wheel. "Dammit!" His voice was raw with anger. "How could they do this?"

"Nick." Whether he wanted her comfort or not, he would get it. She laid a hand on his arm and felt his muscles bunch. "They must have thought it would be the best thing for you."

"Yeah, well, I'm getting damned sick of other people deciding what's the best thing for me. Pam thinks it's best if you and I don't have an affair. My dad and step-mother think it's best if I don't know about the circumstances of my birth. What gives anyone the right to make those choices for someone else?"

"Nothing, I suppose, but if they do it out of love, then maybe you can forgive them."

"I'll work on that." He turned the truck into a narrow lane. "But in the meantime, I'm saying to hell with what Pam thinks. If a casual affair was good enough for my mom and dad, it's good enough for their son." He put on the brakes and turned to her. "We're here."

"At the sacred site?"

"Yes." He switched off the lights. "Look off to your right."

She gazed through the open window and could make out the dull glow of a flat gray-and-white stone as long as the truck and twice as wide. "What kind of rock is that?"

"Granite, with veins of white quartz, polished by years of wind and rain. When the moon's full, the quartz sparkles."

"I'd love to see that."

"Come back sometime and I'll bring you out here again."

She didn't respond to that. Promising a future trip implied a deeper commitment, one neither of them should be making right now. "Let's get out."

"Wait there." Nick opened his door. "I'll come get you."

"I'm capable of—"

"Let me check for critters first." Reaching behind his seat, he pulled out an industrial-size flashlight.

"Oh. Sure. You go right ahead and do that." Her bravado disappeared in no time. "Take your time checking. Do it twice if you want."

The sound of his soft laughter was her reward.

She watched as he walked around, raking the ground with the flashlight beam. When he reached the stone and swept the light over it, she understood what sort of magical effect the moon could create. The white strips of quartz really did sparkle.

He returned to the truck and opened her door. "All clear." He held out his arms.

She moved into them trustingly, allowing him to bracket her waist and lift her to the ground. Once she was standing on the stubby grass, her hands resting on his shoulders, she could feel the heat coming from him in waves.

She glanced into his shadowed face. "This is your show, Nick. Tell me what you need."

"How about some spectacular, purifying sex?"

"You bet." Her body started to hum. "How do you want it?"

"I've been thinking about that. I want to lie naked on my back on that rock."

"Okay." The hum became a roar through her body.

"Then I can look up at the stars, and up at you, riding me for all you're worth."

The roar became a tidal wave of lust. "Come with me." Taking his hand, she led him toward the rock.

9

NICK HAD NEVER BROUGHT a woman out here, and he knew doing it now was taking a chance that Dominique would become an indelible memory. Maybe that wasn't a bad thing. He'd had a shock tonight and she'd been there to offer solace. Remembering her gift to him was the right thing to do whether or not they ever saw each other again after she went home.

But she was here now. Her knees straddling his hips, she sat back and smoothed on the condom. He couldn't choose which sensation to focus on—her tight ass resting on his thighs or her talented hands on his cock.

She looked like a goddess with starlight sprinkled in her short dark hair and glowing on her smooth skin. He caught her spicy scent, which was no longer unfamiliar. The aroma of an aroused Dominique was now imbedded in the pleasure centers of his brain.

He'd expected the rock underneath him to be cold, but it still held warmth from a day in the sun. Or maybe it had absorbed the heat from their bodies, because he felt like a kerosene-soaked torch about to ignite.

She rose up on her knees, and he knew that would be the picture he'd carry with him forever—Dominique in all her naked glory backlit by a sky overflowing with stars. *She belongs here.* He was startled by the clarity of the message.

He'd had insights before in this special place. He understood why the early Shoshones had considered it a sacred site, although few of them came here anymore. But he'd never felt before as if some presence was speaking directly to him. And with such absolute certainty.

Her face was in shadow, but he could just make out the curve of her smile as she leaned toward him and braced a hand on either side of his shoulders. "Is this what you had in mind?" she murmured.

"We're getting there." His words were thick with the unleashed passion that surged through him. He cupped her breasts. "Come closer."

She lowered her breasts to his waiting mouth, and he feasted, savoring the taste of her. He loved the way her breathing changed as he tugged at her nipples. Lost in the wonder of her firm breasts, he almost missed the moment when she lowered her hips just enough to allow his cock the slightest penetration.

Then she withdrew again.

He licked the underside of her breast. "Tease."

"All the best things take time." She sank down again, taking him a little deeper inside her.

Now she had his full attention. The plea rose to his lips before he could censor himself. "More. I want more."

"I know." That smile flashed again as she lifted her hips, abandoning his cock once again.

"Are you trying to torture me?"

"You wanted purifying sex." She eased down halfway before drawing back. "I don't know a lot about such things, but I'm hoping that if I drag this out until you're half-crazy with wanting, we'll generate enough heat to burn away anything that's plaguing you."

He slid both hands down her rib cage so that he could grasp her hips. "I'm already half-crazy. And I want—" he held tight as he surged upward "—this."

She moaned as he made contact with her clit. "Don't blame me if you're not purified."

"I feel purification coming any second." He held her captive with one hand and pressed the thumb of his other right at the spot where they were joined. "How about you?"

She rocked forward against the pressure of his thumb. "I think so."

"Then go for it, Dominique. Go for the burn."

With a whimper she began to move, riding him exactly as he'd fantasized she would, her bottom slapping his thighs, her breasts bouncing with every thrust of her hips.

He would turn into a rocket at any moment, so he kept his thumb where it was and pressed deeper so she'd come with him. She responded with small, frantic cries that increased in volume as her motions became more frenzied. He clenched his jaw, holding on to his climax until it slipped out of his grasp and he came, arching up into her with a bellow of satisfaction.

She bore down and flung herself over the brink with him. Through eyes glazed with lust he watched her in the midst of her orgasm, her back arched, her head flung back, her slender neck exposed. He had the insane urge to rear up and nip at that slender column to mark her.

As they slumped back onto the rock and she nestled her head in the curve of his shoulder, a wolf's howl rose in the clear night air. Another, probably his mate, answered. Nick wrapped his arms around Dominique and smiled. For that moment, with the smooth quartz under them, they'd burned away his anger.

DOMINIQUE WAS GRATEFUL that Nick understood the complicated workings of a tent, because she never would have managed to erect their shelter for the night. She was too exhausted from travel and more sex than she'd ever had in a twenty-four-hour period.

Nick ushered her into the nylon tent and tucked her into the double sleeping bag. She assumed he zipped the tent flap and crawled in beside her, but she had no memory of it because in seconds she was asleep.

She woke up completely disoriented. The light filtering through the rippling turquoise nylon of the tent confused her. She wondered if she'd somehow ended up underwater, although she could still breathe, so that made no sense, and somewhere birds were singing their little hearts out.

Still groggy, she flopped over on her back and her arm nudged warm flesh. Nick's arm, to be precise. She turned her head and discovered he was awake and looking at her, his green eyes clear and untroubled. She took some satisfaction in that.

He smiled. "Good morning."

Rolling to her side, she touched his bristly morning face. "You look happy."

"I am happy. You came through for me, Dominique. I owe you a lot."

"So you're not upset about…everything?"

"I've decided not to think about it for now." He caught her palm and turned his head to place a kiss there.

Amazingly, she reacted as if they'd been apart for weeks. Her pulse quickened and her body grew moist in anticipation of more sex.

But instead of following that kiss with a more intimate touch, Nick squeezed her hand and pushed himself to a sitting position. "Time to get up."

Cold air wafted over her naked body and she burrowed deeper into the sleeping bag. "Maybe not. It's cozy in here, hint, hint."

"Hey, I'm perfectly willing to stay here and play games, but you said you wanted pictures of dawn breaking over this special place."

"I did, didn't I?" She was torn. She might never have this photographic opportunity again, but the thought of heating up the sleeping bag with Nick was irresistible. "It's probably not that important to take the picture."

He laughed. "Yeah, it is." He threw back the top portion of the sleeping bag.

"Yikes!" She tried to grab it back as the icy air gave her goose bumps, but he held it out of reach.

"Come on, Dominique. Please take the damned

picture. I've always wanted a shot of the sun coming up here, but I have no talent for photography. I promise after you record this for posterity we'll come back in here and mess around."

When he put it like that, she could hardly refuse. "Where are my clothes?"

Reaching into a corner of the tent, he picked up a bundle and tossed it at her.

"You're coming out, too, right?" she asked as she began struggling into her panties. She hadn't forgotten about all the critters he'd mentioned last night. For all she knew they stuck around until sunup.

"Absolutely. I'll be the director." He unzipped the flap and picked up his clothes. "See you out there." He crawled from the tent.

Getting dressed in the confined space reminded her of changing clothes in a bathroom stall, except in the stall she was vertical and here she was horizontal. Vertical was better. But she managed it.

When she crawled out into the pearl-colored light of dawn, Nick was waiting with her coat and backpack. He had on a faded denim jacket with the collar turned up. Standing there in the early morning with a shadow of a beard and his hat pulled low over his eyes, he was a walking advertisement for sexy cowboys.

"I brought these from the truck."

She gratefully pulled on her red suede coat. "I can't believe it's so cold this morning when it was so warm last night."

He grinned at her. "Correction. It was effing hot last night."

"Yeah, it was." She gazed at him, mesmerized by how good he looked first thing in the morning. A girl could get used to waking up to a man like Nick. The minute the thought flitted through her mind, she banished it.

Thoughts like that were what had kept her poor and unfocused for so many years. She'd built a solid business doing work she loved. Or mostly loved. She couldn't start all over again.

He handed her the backpack. "I'm not going to tell you how to do your craft, but the sky's getting mighty pretty in the east."

She forced herself to stop looking at him, and concentrate on the landscape instead. The low-lying clouds on the horizon were the color of strawberry sherbet. Even better, the snow on the Tetons reflected the delicate pink.

She'd have been a fool to miss this. "Thank you for booting me out of bed."

"You're welcome."

She pulled out her camera, screwed on a wide-angle lens and snapped a few shots from where they stood. Although she wanted to move around and get different angles, she remembered the routine from last night and hesitated. "Have you checked the area for snakes this morning?"

"They're not awake yet. It needs to be warmer."

"All righty, then. I'm on the move." She walked over and climbed on the smooth rock where they'd had such a memorable time the night before. She took several more pictures from that vantage point, then glanced at Nick.

"I hope what we did last night wasn't disrespectful of this spot."

"Not at all. It's us who have hang-ups about sex. People who are closer to the earth see it as a natural part of their lives. I doubt they would have cared that we used the magic of the stone to..." He paused. "Well, you know. Have a good time."

She wondered what he'd been about to say before he changed his mind. She'd be the first to admit that what they'd shared had been about more than sex. Standing here on the same spot brought back that intense feeling of connection—with Nick, obviously, but with something deeper. If she didn't think it was hokey, she'd say they'd tapped into some kind of cosmic energy.

The magic was still here, pulsing under her feet as she trained her viewfinder on the sky, the mountains, the trees, Nick. He'd turned to look back down the road, and she was able to take several shots of him without his knowledge. Her pictures of daybreak were for him, but the last few were strictly for her.

Yesterday she'd captured him shirtless and virile. This morning he still exuded that broad-shouldered machismo, but his body language telegraphed intense concentration. Zooming in, she focused on the set of his jaw and rigid line of his back. The mood was the polar opposite of the pictures she'd taken the day before.

Walking to a different spot on the rock, she aimed the camera at him and was about to take another photo when he looked over at her. "Someone's coming."

"I don't hear a motor."

"That's because he's on horseback."

She listened more closely and heard the steady rhythm of hoofs on dirt. Judging from Nick's tone of voice he knew exactly who was coming, and had heard the horse long before he'd announced the news to her. It didn't take much imagination on her part to guess who was coming. Even a tenderfoot like her knew that ranch life began at dawn, and Nick hadn't been there.

The hoofbeats grew louder and a rider on a black-and-white paint rounded a bend in the road. Once the horseman saw them he drew back on the reins and slowed to a trot. Dominique didn't know Jack well, but she had no doubt that's who was astride the dramatically marked animal. He would be possessive of the one he chose to ride.

Vaguely she remembered that the animal's black mask had earned him the name Bandit. Bandit had the bearing of a show horse. He pranced forward, tossing his mane and generally looking proud of himself.

Technically speaking, Jack and his horse would make good photography subjects, but she didn't feel like asking him to let her take his picture. From what she'd seen of him so far, she'd bet he would turn her down, anyway.

Rather than walking to meet his brother, Nick stayed put. Dominique decided to do the same. She'd been caught standing on the sacred rock, and wondered if Jack would object to that. If he did, too bad. She'd been invited.

Jack pulled his horse to a halt in front of Nick and swung down from the saddle. He flicked a glance at

Dominique and the tent. "Ma'am." He tugged on the brim of his black Stetson.

He hadn't smiled, so neither did she.

"Hello, Jack."

Nick's wide-legged stance was clearly defiant. "To what do we owe the pleasure of this visit?"

"You weren't at the house. Figured I'd find you out here."

Nick didn't move a muscle. "Seemed like a good night for a campout."

Dominique held her breath and hoped she wouldn't witness a fistfight this morning. Other than in the movies she'd never seen two men fight each other, and she didn't want to now.

"Nick, I know you're upset."

Dominique relaxed a little. Jack's tone held more compassion than she would have expected from him.

"I'm not *upset*." Nick didn't raise his voice, but icy anger infused every syllable. "I'm furious. How dare you keep this from me?"

"It wasn't my secret to tell."

"Granted, but you could have talked him into telling me! You were the heir, his damned namesake. If you'd put the pressure on, he would have caved."

"I tried."

Nick's shoulders bunched under his denim jacket. "The hell you did."

"Believe what you want." Jack turned away and vaulted back onto his horse. "I came out here to tell you not to take it out on Sarah. She doesn't deserve it."

"Doesn't she? I think they call it aiding and abetting."

"It wasn't her secret to tell, either." Jack tightened the reins to control the prancing paint. "You were too young to realize what was happening, but I walked in on a couple of huge fights between them. She begged him to say something when you were old enough to accept the truth, but he swore you'd never have to know."

Nick's chest heaved. "Then she should have told me after he died."

"Oh, yeah? Think about that, Nick. She'd lost the love of her life, and you'd expect her to go against his wishes and tell you she's not your biological mother?"

"I had a right to know, dammit!"

"I hate saying this, but your beef is with a guy who's six feet under. And by the way, I'm pretty sure Calamity Jane's gone into early labor. Just in case you feel like being there." Jack touched the brim of his hat again as he glanced at Dominique. Then he wheeled his horse and galloped back down the road, Bandit's hoofs spitting dust.

Nick stood rooted to the spot as he stared after him. Dominique had no idea what to say. Unfortunately, Jack's explanation made sense. A stubborn man had insisted on fabricating a lie for whatever his reasons—to protect Nick or to protect himself—and love and loyalty had ensured that nobody would betray him.

Nick would have a hard time focusing his anger on the living because they really didn't deserve it, and focusing anger on the dead wouldn't give him much satisfaction. He was in a tough spot, and she hated that for him.

Because she was reluctant to initiate a conversation, and didn't know what else to do, she tucked her camera and lens away and walked over to the tent. Setting her backpack beside it, she reached in and pulled out the double sleeping bag.

After she'd rolled that up the best she could and tied it with the attached strings, she glanced at Jack. He still hadn't moved, so she tackled the tent. It was held up by some bendy poles, and she decided to pull one out of the grommet it was shoved into.

All hell broke loose. She'd had no idea the tent system was spring-loaded. As she tried to grab the collapsing pole, another one popped out of its mooring. The more she tried to corral the poles the faster the tent self-destructed, until it lay in a heap of tangled cords, pole sections and collapsed nylon.

"Need any help?"

A little concerned that this tent mess could be the straw that broke the camel's back, she glanced over her shoulder.

Nick stood behind her grinning.

Thank God. "I was going for helpful but I seem to have created Armageddon."

He nodded. "Pretty much. This could take awhile to untangle."

She groaned. "I'm sorry. I was only—"

"Never mind." Moving around her, he gathered the whole thing into his arms. "I'll deal with it later."

"No, I'll deal with it…except I guess you'll have to be there to show me what to do."

He dumped the tent and its various components in the back of the truck. Then he turned and took her by the shoulders and gazed into her eyes. "Watching you battle it out with that tent made me laugh. Thanks." He gave her a quick, hard kiss on the mouth. "Now we have to go. I have a foal to deliver."

"Can I take pictures?"

He smiled at her. "You bet."

She'd always admired courage under fire, and Nick was demonstrating it in spades. Keeping their relationship within the bounds of a temporary affair was becoming more difficult by the minute.

10

ON THE WAY BACK to the ranch, Nick drove a little faster than was wise and hit some ruts pretty hard. "Sorry."

"It's okay." Dominique held on to the door handle. "I know you want to get there to help with the birth."

"I do. Calamity Jane's my brother Gabe's favorite horse." Nick grimaced. "I suppose now he's technically my half brother."

"Hogwash. He's your brother. Do you suppose he cares about some technicality?"

Nick gave her a quick glance. "Thanks for saying that, even if you don't know Gabe from Adam."

"I don't know him, but I know you. What if the situation were reversed?"

Nick didn't even have to think about it. "I wouldn't give a damn. We're less than a year apart. We grew up almost like twins. Matter of fact, I always thought Jack resented how close Gabe and I were…still are."

"So where is he, exactly?"

Nick steered around a pothole in the road. "He's riding in an event in Colorado."

"Are you going to call him?"

"Once Calamity Jane delivers? You bet. He'd want to know mother and baby were doing well."

"That isn't what I meant."

Nick sighed. "Family skeletons aren't the kind of thing you want to get into over the phone."

"But you said you two are close. Wouldn't he want to know something that important in your life?"

A cottontail darted across the road in front of the truck and Nick slammed on the brakes, throwing both of them hard against the seat belts. "Sorry!"

Dominique settled back against the seat. "No apology necessary. I would have been more upset if you'd run down that bunny."

"Some of the guys call me an old woman because I'll do almost anything to avoid hitting an animal. But I just—"

"You're a vet, Nick. Of course you don't want to see something senselessly maimed or killed."

"No, I don't." He resumed driving, but more slowly than before. Rabbits were always running across the road, and he usually thought more about that. "People have always said I got my soft heart from my mother— well, Sarah."

"You probably did. She probably raised you that way."

"She raised us all that way, but I was the only one who decided to be the champion of all injured or sick animals. I thought it was some genetic thing she passed on." He wanted to be angry with Sarah for that, but she'd never said healing was in his genes. He'd assumed that all on his own.

"Look, I don't have siblings, so I'm probably the last person in the world who should be giving you advice, but I think it would help you to talk with Gabe soon. When's he due home?"

"In about two weeks." Nick slowed to let another rabbit cross the road. "The news can wait until then. He doesn't need to be thinking about something like this when he's out there trying to win events."

"I thought he was showing horses."

"He's on a circuit of cutting horse competitions. It takes plenty of concentration to do well, and every time he wins, it makes the Last Chance horses look that much better to prospective buyers. I don't want to distract him. Nothing will change between now and two weeks from now."

"I still think you should tell him sooner."

Nick's patience, not in the best shape, snapped. "And say what, exactly? 'Hey, Gabe, turns out I'm the kid of some woman named Nicole O'Leary, who got frisky with Dad and then left town. Sorry, don't know a single damned thing about her. Bye.' "

"I'll bet Sarah knows something about her."

Nick pulled up by the barn and killed the motor. "I'm sure she does. But seeing as how she's recently lost my dad, I doubt that would be a cozy conversation, either."

"Maybe not, but you have a lot of unanswered questions, and I would think—"

"Leave it, Dominique." He opened his door before glancing back at her. "This is something I have to handle my way in my own time."

She opened her mouth as if to say something else, but then closed it again. Her dark eyes sparked with anger. "Understood," she said brusquely as she opened the passenger door.

He grabbed her arm. "Look, I know you were there for me when I needed someone desperately, and I appreciate that."

She met his gaze and was obviously still fuming. "Apparently I stepped outside my assigned role. Don't worry. It won't happen again."

"You don't have an assigned role."

"Not anymore, that's for sure. But I think yesterday I did, and you know what? That's okay. It's better, in fact. Keeps everything cleaner."

Knowing he should apologize for being an ass, he couldn't seem to stop himself from continuing to be one. "What about the role you assigned me? When we met, all you wanted was a naked, preferably nameless cowboy!"

Dominique wrenched away from him. "This conversation is over." She jumped down from the truck, grabbed her backpack and ran toward the house.

Nick climbed out and glanced from there to the barn. Butch and Sundance wandered over looking as confused as he felt, their tails wagging slowly, their expressions uncertain. They'd picked up on the tension immediately.

The decision whether to go after Dominique or not was made for him when Jack came running out of the barn. "Thought I heard your truck. Get your butt in here. She's ready to deliver."

DOMINIQUE STORMED UP to the ranch house as if her tail were on fire. How dare Nick speak to her like that? Last night she'd been there to cushion one of the biggest blows he'd ever received in his life, and today he'd essentially told her to stay out of his business.

Her steps slowed. *Wait a minute*. She didn't want to *be* in his business. She didn't want to get so involved with Nick that she wouldn't be able to function happily without him when she returned to her life in Indianapolis.

Those words she'd flung at him in anger just now were absolutely true. Having an assigned role made everything cleaner when the time came to leave. She'd provided a physical outlet for him when he'd needed one. And if she was perfectly honest with herself, she'd admit he'd done the same for her when they'd first met.

She had no right to get on her high horse about any of that, because the arrangement was exactly what she'd hoped for on this trip to Wyoming—hot cowboy sex. How Nick handled telling his news was so not her business, and he'd had the good sense to tell her to back off.

If she could remember to keep her relationship opinions to herself, they could enjoy each other's bodies without worrying about messy emotions.

In the meantime, she was missing a golden opportunity to photograph the birth of a foal, something she'd never seen. Spinning on her heel, she hurried back down to the barn.

Butch and Sundance where lying in the sun just outside the door, as if stationed there.

"Hi, guys."

They glanced up, thumped their tails in greeting, and put their heads back on their paws. Dominique had the distinct impression Nick had told them to stay right where they were until he showed up again.

She ducked through the doorway into the coolness of the barn. Yesterday afternoon she'd roamed the ranch snapping pictures of paint horses romping in the pasture and Emmett schooling a cutting horse. Then she'd prowled through the barn looking for artsy shots of stall doors and tack hanging from pegs.

She'd stopped by Calamity Jane's stall, but even if she hadn't scoped out the situation yesterday, she'd have figured it out, because of the group of ranch hands hanging around offering advice.

Dominique looked for Emmett before remembering he had the day off and might even be going on a picnic later today with Pam. Probably just as well he wasn't here, considering that he'd been in on the conspiracy to keep the details of Nick's birth secret. Nick might not be ready to see the foreman just yet.

"Hey, Jack, you said the show was gonna start, but I don't see nothin' yet," commented one lanky cowboy with red hair sticking out from under his hat. The guy looked no more than twenty-two.

Slipping her camera out of her backpack, Dominique approached the group and stood next to a short, older man with a graying handlebar mustache.

She could hear the murmurs of Jack and Nick and the heavy breathing of the horse, but she couldn't see anything. Finally she tapped the older man on the arm and asked softly, "What's going on?"

He glanced at her. "Oh, Calamity Jane's just taking her time, is all. Everything's under control now that the doc's here."

"That's good to know." Despite herself, she was impressed with the fact that the cowboy referred to Nick as "the doc." She hadn't seen him work in that capacity. She only knew him in connection with manual labor and sweaty sex.

The cowboy looked at the camera in her hand and moved aside. "Go on up so you can take some pictures."

"But then you won't be able to see as well."

"I've watched this process a bunch of times. It's always a thrill, though. You'll be glad you're here."

Dominique thanked him and moved into his spot. The stall door was open so the cluster of men surrounding it could see in. Predictably, the mare was another paint—a reddish-brown color with white splotches. She lay on her side in a bed of straw, her flanks heaving, while Jack stroked her neck. Nick, wearing long rubber gloves, crouched at the business end. A medical bag sat next to him.

Dominique felt a rush of pride watching him as he prepared to help deliver this foal. He'd draped his jacket over the side of the stall and rolled his sleeves up past his elbows. He wore his straw hat, but he'd pushed it back on his head so it wouldn't interfere with the job he was doing. He was intent on his task and probably had no idea she was there.

He wouldn't expect her to be there, in fact, after the way they'd parted. While Jack continued to stroke the mare's neck, Nick talked to her in soothing tones. From where Dominique stood she couldn't make out the words, but there was no mistaking the comforting quality of Nick's voice.

She had a sudden image of him in the delivery room for the birth of his child. He wouldn't be the guy turning green or running for the nearest exit. Nick would hang in there and do what he could to help the woman he loved deliver their baby. Now that he knew his own mother hadn't had that kind of support, likely he'd be even more committed to giving it.

Raising the camera, Dominique took a picture of Nick as he knelt down to get a better look. "We're there, Jack," he said distinctly. "Come on, Janey, girl. You can do it."

The horse moved her legs restlessly and gave a little groan as something transparent and blue poked out from her hindquarters.

"That's it," Nick crooned. "Hang in there, sweetheart."

At first Dominique wasn't sure what she was looking at, but then she realized the foal, covered in the fetal membrane, was emerging like a swimmer making a dive, front feet straight out and head resting on its forelegs.

"Give her a little help, Nick," Jack said.

"Don't want to steal her thunder." Nick had a smile in his voice.

"Somehow I don't think she'd mind." Jack sounded as cheerful as Dominique had ever heard him.

"Nick's getting lazy in his old age," teased the cowboy with the red hair.

"Okay." Nick grasped the foal's front legs. "Janey, I know you can do this all by yourself, but everybody else thinks you need an assistant." As the horse wheezed and groaned, he carefully began to tug the foal free.

Dominique took a couple of pictures, but then simply watched in awe as the wet, gangly foal gradually emerged, helped along by Nick's strong, capable hands. The muscles in his arms bunched from the effort, and Dominique held her breath, waiting with everyone else.

When the mare gave one last push and the foal tumbled to the straw, Dominique was swamped with a rush of unexpected emotion. Feeling silly, she blinked and took a deep breath. Maybe it wasn't so silly. She'd never seen a baby being born.

"It's a boy!" Nick announced to the onlookers. "And I'm pretty sure he's a paint!" A cheer went up from the assembled group.

Calamity Jane struggled to her feet, hobbled over to the foal and began licking him clean. Both Jack and Nick stood, too, and Nick pretended he was going to wipe his gloved hands on Jack's shirt.

Laughing, Jack dodged out of his reach. Nick pulled off the slimy gloves and dumped them in a nearby bucket.

"Congratulations, cowboy." Jack slapped Nick on the back. "He's a beauty. Black markings just like his daddy."

"Yeah, he is a good-looking foal. Gabe'll go ape-shit over this little guy."

Dominique couldn't see Nick's face, but she had to believe he was wearing a wide grin. The dramatic change in the relationship between Nick and Jack fascinated her. An hour ago these two had been facing off, tempers at the boiling point. Now they were buds sharing in a special moment.

"There he goes," announced the red-haired cowboy. "He's standing up!"

Instinct took over as Dominique raised her camera and recorded the determined efforts of the trembling, knock-kneed foal as he tried to get all four legs under him. He was minutes old, and he was...standing!

Another cheer went up, and this time Dominique joined in. She was no longer embarrassed by the lump in her throat. She'd never witnessed anything quite like this tiny miracle, and she wouldn't need pictures to help her remember it.

"So you came after all."

She glanced up to find Nick less than two feet away. She'd been so focused on taking shots of the new baby she hadn't realized he'd walked in her direction. Her pulse rate jumped.

"I wouldn't have missed it for the world," she said.

He adjusted his hat so it tilted lower over his eyes. "That wasn't the impression I got when you stomped up to the house."

She glanced around and discovered nobody was paying much attention to them. Everyone was hanging over the stall admiring the new addition to the Last Chance Ranch. "I came to my senses," she said.

"I'm glad you had a chance to see that." His gaze was steady but unreadable. "Did you get enough pictures?"

"Yes." She no longer knew where they stood, and the conversation had taken an uncomfortable turn. "Nick, I was out of line to be telling you what you should do about Gabe. I apologize."

He hesitated a minute, as if choosing his words carefully. "I was wrong, too. You can't ask a person to help you through a rough patch and then refuse to listen to some well-meaning advice."

"But you're right that it's none of my business."

Remorse flickered in his green eyes. "I'm not so sure about that, Dominique. I mean, when you're willing to brave snakes and bears for me, I owe you the courtesy of listening to what you have to say."

"You listened and decided against my suggestion. I shouldn't have kept trying to make my case."

"Why did you?"

Now there was a question she didn't want to answer. A truthful reply would mean admitting that she was invested in his welfare, that she'd begun to care for him far more than someone only interested in a fun romp should.

"Hey, Nick!" called the red-haired cowboy. "Jack says you've got some cigars stashed away for this occasion."

Dominique was grateful for the reprieve. "Sounds like you need to help some people celebrate."

"Maybe." He gave her another searching glance before turning toward the men grouped around the stall. "I have a few cigars tucked away, Jeb, but with the schedule we've all been keeping lately, you won't have time to smoke 'em."

Jack groaned. "Pass out the damned cigars."

"Be right there, then." Nick faced Dominique. "I gotta go. I'm assuming you don't want a cigar."

"Thanks, but I gave them up last year."

His soft laugh stroked her nerve endings and made her long for a different kind of celebration.

As if reading her mind, he touched her cheek. "If you won't take a cigar, how about dinner tonight?"

"I'd love it." Warmth flooded her at the thought that they'd healed the breach between them. Her next thought, that her excitement over his invitation should probably serve as a warning that she was slowly falling under his spell, she shoved aside.

"Great. Be ready by seven, and wear your dancing shoes."

"I'm not much of a dancer."

His eyes twinkled. "No worries. I am."

11

NICK DISTRIBUTED THE cigars, but shoved his in his shirt pocket. Although he was thrilled about the birth, he wasn't in the mood to sit around the barn and talk about it.

Jack had already made his excuses and headed out, claiming a watering trough was malfunctioning. Nick was relieved to see him go. The new foal, which they'd named Calamity Sam, had briefly distracted Jack from his grief and guilt, but Nick had watched the familiar black cloud settle over his brother as the minutes passed. It was hard to believe he used to be a hell of a lot of fun.

Once outside the barn, Nick gave each of the dogs a biscuit from his pocket as a reward for waiting quietly during the birth. They accepted the treat and joyously returned to their usual occupation of chasing rabbits and squirrels. Nick watched them bound off, and then headed toward the house.

As he climbed the steps to the porch, he tried to decide whether to take a shower first or phone Gabe.

Before finding the letter from his birth mother, he wouldn't have thought twice about calling his younger brother. Things were different now.

He'd started playing the if-only game—never a good idea, but he couldn't seem to help himself. If only he hadn't volunteered to go through his dad's trunk, he'd still be blissfully ignorant. His only problems would be whether or not he was falling for the bodacious Dominique, and how the heck he could alter Jack's attitude.

Those problems had seemed unmanageable, but this one… He still couldn't get his mind around it. If only he'd reacted differently. Destroyed the letter and pretended he'd never seen it… But he wasn't made that way. His father had been, apparently.

Nick was still thinking about his dad's secretive nature and the coming phone conversation with Gabe as he entered the house and climbed the stairs to the second floor. The place was quiet except for the sound of water running. Dominique must be showering.

Roni's room had an attached bath, something Sarah had insisted on because Roni was a teenage girl in a houseful of men, and had needed her privacy. She'd cherished that room.

She'd been fourteen when Emmett had found her hitchhiking, running away from an abusive father. After the foreman convinced her to come to the ranch, she'd tried to steal a truck, but instead of turning her over to the police, Emmett and Jonathan had decided to hire her to keep the ranch trucks running.

These days Roni traveled the country in her capacity as a NASCAR team mechanic, so she was hardly ever home. That made her room with its attached bath perfect for guests. Nick didn't have that kind of convenience. He still had to cross the hall.

As he passed Roni's room he heard Dominique start to sing. And man, was she terrible at it! He recognized the words to "Zippity Do-Da," or he wouldn't have had the slightest idea what she was trying to sing.

Obviously, she either didn't know or didn't care that she had no talent for the activity, because she was belting out the lyrics as if someone had just signed her to a recording contract. Nick stood there, shaking his head and smiling. Dominique was a kick. If she danced as horribly as she sang, his toes would be in for a beating tonight.

But tonight seemed a long way away. Dominique, however, was very close, and at the moment very naked. He shoved his hand in his jeans pocket, and sure enough, found a condom left in there.

He tried the bedroom door and wasn't surprised that she hadn't locked it. But he didn't want to scare her to death or call up the scene from *Psycho*. As he opened the door, he began singing along with her, although his version was actually in tune.

She stopped singing abruptly. "Nick? Is that you?"

"It's me." He walked to the door of the bathroom and peeked in. The space was steamy and smelled like fresh flowers. The NASCAR-themed shower curtain drawn across the tub was opaque so he couldn't see her. "Can I come in?"

She poked her head around the curtain, drawing it under her chin so he still couldn't see anything but her wet hair and face. Drops of water clung to her long eye-lashes. She looked like a wood sprite, or what he imagined a wood sprite would look like if they existed.

"It seems you're already in," she said. "Is anything wrong?"

"No." Unless he counted his growing need to be with her 24/7. "I was heading to take a shower when I heard you…singing."

She grinned. "Nice of you to call it that. I've been told I sound like an alley cat in heat."

"I was thinking more of a bull moose."

"See, none of my friends have heard one of those, so they had to go with the alley cat comparison." She continued to gaze at him as if trying to figure out why he'd shown up in her bathroom in the middle of the day. "Did you want to talk? I'll be through in a couple of minutes."

"Actually, I could use a shower first."

"Okay. I can hang around upstairs until you're finished with that. Just come on back to my room. I'll be here."

"Seems a shame to have to walk all the way down the hall to take that shower. It'll just waste time."

Understanding slowly dawned on her expressive face as he added, "I thought you might be willing to share yours."

"Nick, it's the middle of the day. What if some-one—"

"I know the rhythm of the people who live in this house. Nobody's likely to come up here for at least a couple of hours, if then."

Her eyes darkened and her breathing changed so subtly that an unobservant person might not have noticed.

But he did. "Can I take silence for a yes?"

"I think you're a really bad boy, Nick Chance."

He began stripping off his clothes. "And I think you like it."

"I suppose I do." She eased the shower curtain back a few inches.

It wasn't enough to let water out, but gave him an excellent view of her standing there, wet and glistening in the glare of the overhead light.

Holding his gaze, she slowly rubbed a washcloth over her breasts. "Ready for some good, clean fun?"

He set a world record getting undressed, but remembered to pull the condom out of his jeans pocket. Heart thundering with anticipation, he walked over to the tub.

As she moved aside and made room for him under the spray, she glanced at the condom in his hand and laughed softly. "Not exactly subtle, are we?"

"No pockets."

"I'll take care of that." Plucking the condom packet from his hand, she set it in the recessed soap dish. Then she lathered up the washcloth and glanced into his eyes. "Where would you like me to start?"

His vocal cords felt tight because he wanted her so much, but he managed a reply. "Use your imagination." He could say that to her and know all kinds of wonderful things would happen. He had enough experience to realize that wasn't so easy to find in a woman. But he had it now, with Dominique, and he'd be wise to take this one day, one hour, one minute at a time.

She applied the soapy cloth to his chest and then took the time to wash each of his arms. When she returned to his pecs and began circling gradually lower, he decided the present was a very good place to be. Any second now she'd arrive at the destination he had in mind for her. Almost there. Almost… Or maybe not.

He should have expected her to tease him. That was part of what made her more exciting than any other woman he'd had sex with. She'd deliberately avoided his erect penis and aching balls. Instead she moved to his thighs. As she knelt down to wash them thoroughly, her mouth was *right there*.

She seemed oblivious to the opportunity. Instead, she moved lower, out of range, and washed his calves. He wondered if a man could go insane waiting for a woman to touch his johnson.

After washing his feet, she stood. "All done!"

"You missed a place."

"Your back! Turn around and I'll wash it."

Yes, a man could go insane. "I don't care about my back."

"Then I'm not sure what you're…oh, maybe you mean this part?" She lightly touched his dick with the washcloth.

Nick clenched his jaw to make sure he didn't come right then and there. "That's part of what I meant."

"And maybe this part." She massaged his balls with the soft terry cloth.

He drew in a breath and closed his eyes. "Yeah."

"I'm so forgetful."

"Like hell."

"But I'll take care of everything." She wrapped the washcloth around his penis and began to rub up and down.

He groaned with pleasure. Too much pleasure. If she kept that up…

"Let's rinse you off." She splashed warm water on him. "And lick you dry." Kneeling in the tub, she began doing things with her hands and tongue that were guaranteed to make him explode.

He cupped her head, his fingers making a squeaking sound in her clean wet hair. He wasn't sure whether to stop her or urge her on. Coming now would feel so good, but coming later, buried inside her, would feel great, too. If they had more time together he'd be able to enjoy both options.

But he didn't have that luxury. Straining with the effort to hold back, he drew her to her feet. It seemed like forever since he'd kissed this woman, and he needed to taste her. Then he needed to roll on a condom and create that elemental connection with her. When they were locked together, moving as one, his world made sense.

Their kiss was hotter than a blacksmith's forge. Vaguely, he realized the shower was turning cool, but he didn't care. His focus was her mouth, her breasts, her clit.

He hated to stop touching and kissing her long enough to put on the condom, but sacrifices had to be made. It wasn't the easiest maneuver because he was shaking. At last he was able to cup her firm ass in both hands, lift her up against the tiled wall and sink into her.

They were both slippery as eels and she had trouble keeping her legs wrapped around his hips. She began to laugh, which wasn't what he was going for.

"It's not funny," he muttered as he braced a foot against each side of the tub and began to pump.

She grinned at him. "Just so you know, if you drop me, there will be hell to pay."

"I won't drop you. Lock your ankles together."

"I've tried. They keep sliding apart. You'd better make this fast."

"It would be my pleasure." He picked up the pace and took satisfaction in the way her laughter faded and her eyes darkened. When her breathing grew ragged and her fingers bit into his shoulders, he knew he had her.

"How's that?" he asked conversationally, although it took all the lung control he possessed to keep from gasping while he said it.

"Passable."

"You are such a liar." He rushed the words because soon he wouldn't be able to say anything. "You're going to come any second."

"Think so?" She gripped him tighter and licked her lips.

"I know so." He made sure he slid in hard and tight with each stroke.

At last she began to whimper.

"Told you." He watched her eyes, and knew the moment was upon her when they widened. She gave one sharp cry, and her spasms rolled over his cock. He was ready, so ready, and her climax was all he needed to send him surging forward in a shuddering, pulsing release.

Gasping, he rested his forehead against hers. "That was…great…."

"Mmm." She sagged against the tile and gulped air.

"If I smoked cigars…now would be the time."

"Same here."

"Wonder if we'll ever do it in a bed."

"Might be easier."

"Tonight. My bed." He'd bought it last year from a guy in Shoshone who made hand-carved bed frames. So far Nick had been the only person in that bed, but that was about to change.

Thinking about it now wasn't a good idea, though, because he started to get hard again. He was fresh out of condoms, and besides, sooner or later someone would come looking for him. Just his luck it would be Jack… again.

DOMINIQUE LOANED NICK a towel to wrap around his hips so he could walk down the hall to his room without flashing anyone who might show up. He insisted on sticking the unlit cigar between his teeth before he left.

Fortunately, no one came along, because Nick's exit from her room wearing a towel, carrying his clothes and clenching a cigar between his teeth would pretty much tell the story of what had just happened. She couldn't resist watching him go, even though she looked equally incriminating wrapped in the mate to the towel he wore.

When he reached his room, he turned and gave her a wave and a salute with his cigar. She wished she'd thought to grab her camera. Then again, recording all these stolen moments might not be such a good idea if she wanted to keep this affair from taking on added significance.

Once he was safely through the door of his room, she ducked back inside hers. She took another quick shower in what was now cold water, dried off and put on jeans and a fitted red T-shirt. Before Nick left, she'd almost asked him if he'd called his brother yet, but she'd restrained herself. What he said or didn't say to Gabe was not her concern. She didn't even know the guy, probably wouldn't ever meet him. And that was the end of that.

In the same vein, she vowed not to corral Mary Lou after lunch and pepper her with questions. This morning when Nick had mentioned that the ranch house cook had probably been in on the conspiracy, Dominique had realized she could be a source of information. Nick probably wouldn't ask, but Dominique could. But she wouldn't.

Although she couldn't help being curious about Nick's mother, her curiosity would have to go unsatisfied. She had a hot cowboy who wanted to have sex with her at every opportunity. End of story.

She was about to turn on the hair dryer when her cell phone played "Back Home Again in Indiana," her parents' assigned ring. She'd called them yesterday to say she'd arrived safely and was transferring to the Last Chance Ranch. She'd promised to give them a call today and let them know how everything was going, but between the sex and…well, the *sex,* she'd totally forgotten.

When she answered, her mother sounded miffed.

"Sorry, Mom. It's so gorgeous here that I got caught up in admiring the scenery." Now that was absolutely true.

"Your father and I went online and looked up the Last Chance Ranch," her mom said. "It's quite an operation. The land must be worth a bundle."

"I haven't paid much attention to the business side of the ranch, Mom." Dominique tried not to be irritated with her mother's constant emphasis on the bottom line. But it had been a sore point for years.

Dominique was fairly sure her father hated his corporate management job, had hated it for a long time, but it paid well, and her mother wouldn't hear of him quitting. It was no wonder Dominique's artistic temperament had driven her mom crazy.

When Herman arrived on the scene and shepherded Dominique into the wedding and portrait end of the photography business, her mother had been overjoyed. At last her daughter had a decent bottom line.

For her part, Dominique had discovered that having a steady income wasn't the equivalent of going to hell, and she'd decided not to reject the concept simply to rebel against her mother. The success of Jeffries Studio was an unexpected source of pride, and she was finally free of her admonitions to find something lucrative. Even so, Dominique was sick of her mom's preoccupation with the almighty dollar.

"You might be wise to pay attention to the business

side of that ranch," her mother said now. "Who's their photographer? Somebody's making a bundle taking pictures of those gorgeous horses for the Web site. It could be you."

"I'm on vacation, Mom. I'm not here to rustle up business." Dominique couldn't imagine approaching Nick about becoming the ranch's official photographer. "I'm sure they have someone local."

"Your dad and I both agree that whoever they use doesn't have your eye."

Dominique groaned. "Whoever they use probably lives around here, which means they don't have to pay to fly them out. It's a Web site. The pictures don't have to be portrait quality."

"Yes, but what if they were? What if you provided the kind of photos that could be mounted on canvas and hung over the mantel? People who pay thousands for a horse would probably pay dearly for a portrait of that horse. You could divide the profits with the ranch. Win-win."

"You're giving me a headache, Mom."

"You always say that when I suggest a way to grow your business."

"Seriously, I'm here to relax. That whole thing with Herman was damned painful, and—"

"I know it was, dear. We're as shocked as everyone else. But you have to admit that despite all that, he was good for you. It didn't work out in the end, but you wouldn't have Jeffries Studio if he hadn't pushed you to create a solid business model."

Dominique gritted her teeth. "I do admit that. But for

this vacation, I want to forget about freaking Herman, and I even want to forget about the freaking studio, okay?"

"No need to get hostile, Dominique."

"I'm sorry, Mom." Instantly she regretted her outburst. She did love her studio. She did. Except sometimes she thought if she had to work another wedding, she'd go drown herself in the Wabash River.

12

NICK KEPT MEANING TO CALL Gabe and tell him about the foal. He really did. But by the time he'd gone back to the barn to check on Calamity Jane and Calamity Sam so he could give his brother an update, lunchtime had rolled around. Might as well wait until after to make the call.

Jack wasn't in the dining room when he walked in, and neither was Emmett. But of course Emmett wasn't there. If Pam had succeeded in her campaign, he was off somewhere having a picnic.

Just as well. Nick was conflicted about Emmett. Realistically, the guy couldn't have defied his boss and risked his job to tell Nick about his parentage, but Nick wished he had taken that chance and done it, anyway. For Emmett's sake, he would have kept his mouth shut. Over the years he'd come to think of him as a second father.

Emmett could have taken him fishing some lazy summer day and filled him in. They would have made a pact never to tell anyone that Nick knew the truth. And that would have been that. Yeah, Nick could have lived with that scenario.

Dominique had come in ahead of him and her table was already filled with cowhands. He allowed himself a brief moment to imagine what life would be like if she stuck around. He'd have to beat guys off with a stick, but that would be okay. More than okay. But he dared not let himself hope that she'd change her mind about staying in Indiana.

Derailing that train of thought, he grabbed a chair at another table, where Jeb and Watkins were chowing down on spareribs and coleslaw. "Guess you guys arrived too late to sit with the lady, huh?"

Watkins laughed and stroked his mustache. "She's a looker, all right. I gave her my spot this morning so's she could take pictures of the foaling. Seems nice enough. What do you say, Jeb?"

The young cowboy's face turned as red as his hair. "She's okay."

Watkins punched him on the arm. "Come on, boy. You were drooling over her and you know it."

Nick decided enough was enough. "I'm taking her to dinner at the Spirits and Spurs tonight."

"Oh." Jeb looked crestfallen.

Watkins patted him on the shoulder. "Take comfort in the fact you have excellent taste, son."

"Here you go, Nick." Mary Lou appeared with a plate of ribs and coleslaw. "Congratulations." She put the dish in front of him. "Heard about Calamity Sam."

"Thanks, Mary Lou." He glanced up at her. "Heard anything else interesting lately?"

Her expression was cautious. "Like what?"

"Oh, I don't know. Just anything out of the ordinary."

"I have no idea what you're talking about, Nick Chance. Now, eat your lunch."

He thought she knew exactly what he was talking about. Jack had probably alerted her that the cat was out of the bag, and now she was waiting to see what Nick planned to do next. For the time being, he'd eat his meal. He had skipped breakfast and was hungrier than a bear coming out of hibernation.

Logically, he should be angry with Mary Lou, who also could have told him about the circumstances of his birth. She'd been here as long as Emmett.

But Mary Lou would never have done anything to upset Sarah. Those two women stood together on issues with more solidarity than most married couples he knew. If Sarah hadn't wanted Nick to know about his mother, Mary Lou wouldn't have betrayed that trust.

Emmett was another story. He and Nick's father had locked horns several times over the years, sort of the way the foreman now locked horns with Jack. Jack was more like their dad than either Nick or Gabe. Nick could look at him, especially now that Jack was in charge of the ranch, and see their dad reincarnated. Jonathan Chance had been stubborn, moody, and for some reason that Nick didn't get, like catnip to women.

Watson picked up his napkin and wiped his mustache before addressing Nick. "I s'pose by now you've called Gabe about Calamity Sam."

Nick finished one rib and picked up another. "You

know, I haven't had a chance yet." A picture of Dominique naked in the shower made him glance down at his plate to hide the self-satisfied smile that threatened to break out.

"You haven't?" Jeb sounded amazed. "He said to call the minute Janey dropped that foal."

Nick dredged up another excuse. "I figure this time of day he's in the middle of an event and wouldn't even get the call."

"You could leave him a message," Jeb said. "You could phone now and then Watkins and me, we could yell out, 'It's a boy!' Gabe would get a kick out of that."

Nick wiped his hands and picked up a fork to tackle the coleslaw. "Don't have my phone with me."

"Use mine." Jeb unclipped a cell phone from his belt and slid it across the table.

"Cell phones." Watkins shook his head. "A self-respecting cowboy does *not* carry a cell phone. It's unnatural."

"It's the modern age," Jeb said. "Might as well get used to it, Watkins. For all you know, Jack's gonna require us all to carry them."

"God, I hope not. I hate those damn things." Watkins stared at the phone on the table. "But as long as the contraption's among us, I say you call Gabe on it, Nick. He'd appreciate it, even if you just leave him a message."

Nick realized this could be a way out of his dilemma. "Sure, why not?" He picked up the phone and punched in Gabe's cell number.

Nick hated to inform Watkins, but all the Chance

men had been carrying cell phones for years. They weren't requiring it of their cowhands yet, but the day might come. A few, like Watkins, would resist. Emmett wouldn't be crazy about the idea, either.

"Listen, Jeb," Watkins said as he glared at the red-head next to him, "we're not doing that tomfool thing you came up with, either, yelling, 'It's a boy!' It's not dignified."

"I think it would be cool," Jeb countered.

Watkins snorted. "Cool like carrying a cell phone clipped to your belt like some geek from Silicon Valley? I need to educate you on the tradition of the American cowboy, son. We're strong, we're silent and we don't carry an effing cell phone."

Jeb lifted his chin. "I do."

Nick had to give the kid props. He didn't back down from Watkins's bluster. As Nick listened to the phone ring on Gabe's end, he hoped his brother would answer. He couldn't be expected to tell Gabe about his discovery in the middle of the lunchroom. But leaving a message meant Gabe would call back, and then Nick wouldn't feel so great about omitting critical info from the conversation.

Just his luck, the call went to voice mail. "Hey, Gabe!" Nick pumped enthusiasm into his message. "We're celebrating today, buddy-boy, because Calamity Jane delivered a spanking new colt. We named him Calamity Sam, but if that doesn't work for you, we haven't done the paperwork yet so there's time to change it. I hope you're kicking butt out there!"

"It's a boy!" Jeb called out, as Watkins cringed and muttered something under his breath.

"That was Jeb," Nick said. "Obviously, he's a happy man. Wish you were here to smoke a cigar with us. Talk to you later, bro." He snapped the phone shut and handed it back. "Thanks."

"You're welcome. I'll bet Gabe is going to be happy when he hears that message," Jeb stated.

"I'm sure he will be." *And then he'll call me back.* Nick wasn't ready for that. Although generally speaking he missed having Gabe around, he was grateful that his brother wasn't here.

DOMINIQUE WASN'T SURE what people considered proper dancing shoes out here in the West, but she'd decided the boots she'd bought back in Indiana would have to do. Western wear was in style these days, so even in Indianapolis she'd found boots, boot-cut jeans and outfits decorated with fringe.

She'd packed a white circle skirt that would flare out nicely if Nick twirled her on the dance floor tonight. Her skirt might be the only thing that would make her look like a dancer, because her moves had never been very good. And after two years with Herman, she was extra rusty, because her boyfriend didn't dance.

As she dressed for the evening, adding a green plaid Western shirt tied at her midriff, she thought of what Herman would have said about this outfit. *It's so obviously trendy. You'd be better off investing in something classic.*

"Get out of my head, Herman," she muttered. "You're

a jerk and I'm not living by your rules anymore." Or mostly not. He'd taught her to balance a checkbook, and encouraged her to set up an IRA. She needed to keep some of that discipline in her life.

As she transferred a few essentials from her big purse to a little fringed shoulder bag she'd brought for exactly this kind of evening, she found the stapled together sheets of paper that comprised her e-mailed ticket confirmation.

She forced herself to look at it as a reminder that four days from now she'd be back in Indianapolis. Nick would be here taking care of the new foal and figuring out how to handle the recently revealed circumstances of his birth. They would be leading separate lives, which was as it should be.

But thinking about that separation made her tummy clench. That wasn't good. It meant the light and carefree fling she'd hoped for wasn't going according to plan. She was bonding with Nick and perhaps even bonding with this place.

As she put on her makeup, she allowed herself to think of what would happen if she decided to leave Indianapolis and move here. Economic disaster, that's what. Although Shoshone was still a sleepy little town, Jackson, where she'd landed two days ago, was far from sleepy.

Nick hadn't been kidding about Hollywood types coming to Jackson Hole. And where there was Hollywood money, there would be a horde of folks offering services exactly like hers. Well-known photographers probably summered there. Dominique might like to imagine she'd be competing with small-town amateurs, but that would be naive.

Not that her host had asked her to pull up stakes and move here—far from it. When she'd made it clear that she would be going home and the affair would be officially over at that point, he'd been fine with the news. She wasn't a cowgirl or a ranch woman, and he obviously realized that. Once he found out she had no talent for the two-step, he'd really know she wasn't cut out for this life.

At least she apparently hadn't lost her talent for sex. That was good to know, after two unimaginative years with Herman. She dabbed her spicy cologne behind her ears and into her cleavage. For good measure she lifted her skirt and patted a little on the inside of each thigh. She might be a liability on the dance floor, but she'd make up for it once she arrived in his bed.

At precisely seven he rapped on her bedroom door. She opened it to discover that he'd traded his straw cowboy hat for a black Stetson that made him look vaguely dangerous. His green shirt, cut in the Western style, matched his eyes, and his jeans showed off the body she had grown to know and love. His polished silver-and-turquoise belt buckle was better than a neon sign. Her fantasy cowboy had come through for her again.

His gaze swept over her outfit. "I like it."

"Don't be fooled. I may look as if I could two-step into the night, but I truly am a klutz on the dance floor."

He smiled. "I'll bet you're the sexiest klutz in the place."

"Just give me a couple of beers and I'll fake it. That always worked for me in college."

"I really don't care if you can dance." When he slipped his arms around her waist the pearl snaps at his cuffs rubbed tantalizingly against the bare skin of her midriff.

"That's good, because I can't."

"I just want to get you hot and bothered." He pulled her closer.

She breathed in the scent of a shaved and showered Nick, and decided she liked that version almost as much as the sweaty one. "You've already accomplished that. Should we raid the kitchen and stay home?"

"No." He gave her a quick kiss and guided her toward the stairs. "This is your vacation, and it wouldn't be complete without spending one evening in a honky-tonk drinking beer and making some attempt at the two-step."

She wished he hadn't mentioned that she was on vacation. But maybe he'd done it on purpose, to remind them both that this happy little situation was only temporary. If she was smart, she'd keep her plane reservation information out on her nightstand to make sure she didn't forget.

She probably wasn't very smart, because as Nick helped her into the old ranch truck, which looked suspiciously as if he'd washed it sometime this afternoon, she refused to believe this would be the only time she'd go out two-stepping with Nick Chance.

THE ROAD INTO SHOSHONE ran past the Bunk and Grub, and Nick glanced over at the small parking lot beside the B and B. "Emmett's truck is still there. The picnic must have extended into dinner."

Dominique didn't look surprised. "You do know that Pam has a thing for Emmett, right?"

"Sort of, I guess. I wasn't really positive until she came up with that picnic idea."

"I think they look good together."

Nick thought about it. "Maybe, but it's not that simple." He slowed the truck as the only stoplight in town turned red. "This always happens. How can I continually hit the red? There's not another vehicle in sight. I'm always tempted to run it, but sure as I did, Elmer, who owns the gas station on that far corner, would report me to the county sheriff's office."

"You're kidding."

"Nope. Elmer campaigned to get this light so people would be more likely to slow down and think about buying gas. He's not about to let us pretend it isn't there."

Dominique laughed. "Are you sure he doesn't have a remote control for that light? That way he could guarantee that it's always red when someone pulls up to the intersection."

"I never thought of that. I don't know if it's even possible, but he's into electronic gizmos, so he might have figured out a way to control that light. All I know is that once you're caught, you sit here forever."

"That's fine. Gives me a chance to check out the town."

"Which is laid out right in front of you." Nick waved his hand. "One block of businesses in each of the four directions. You've got your bank, your feed store, your post office, your combo barbershop and beauty parlor, your small grocery, your ice cream parlor, the Shoshone Diner for daytime food and the Spirits and Spurs for the evenings. Pretty basic stuff."

"Sometimes basic is good. When I walk into one of those big malls, I feel as if I have too many choices. Mostly I leave without buying anything."

He found that encouraging. She might not be as tied to Indianapolis as he'd thought. "So why not simplify your life and move to the country?" he asked as the light finally changed and he drove through the intersection.

"Because I'd starve to death. I need a good-size urban population to support my studio."

He had no answer for that because the way she'd told him her photography business was structured now, she was probably right. Yet he'd had the feeling all along that given the choice, she'd go back to shooting artistic photos if she could find a way to pay the bills.

She sighed wistfully. "You must have had fun growing up here, though. I'll bet you know most of the people in town."

"Yep. Gabe and I sometimes spent the weekends with our grandma Judy. Jack would never come, said it was baby stuff, but he didn't know what he was missing. She'd spoil us rotten. She…" He trailed off as he realized that Grandma Judy was Sarah's mother, which made her no blood relation at all. Maybe Jack hadn't come because he'd felt like an outsider. Now it was Nick's turn to feel as if he didn't quite belong.

"Nick, she's still your grandmother," Dominique said gently, as if she'd read his mind.

"Not technically. My dad was an only child and both his parents have passed on. For all I know, I have no living blood relatives left."

"Of course you do. You have two half brothers."

"You know, I used to think the same thing when Jack would make a comment that sounded as if he didn't feel part of the family. I get it, now." Nick pulled the truck into the parking lot of the Spirits and Spurs.

Dominique glanced at him. "But you had a father who wanted you to be a part of the family and accept his new wife as your mother. You've admitted she treated each of you boys the same."

"Yes, but in her heart of hearts—"

"In her heart of hearts she loved you, Nick. I can guarantee it. If she hadn't you wouldn't have turned out to be the compassionate person you are."

He switched off the motor and turned to gaze at her. "I'm not feeling all that compassionate about this secret they kept from me."

Dominique unbuckled her seat belt and turned to him. "It may take time," she said softly. "But there's a bedrock of goodness in you, and I have a sneaky suspicion that Sarah had quite a bit to do with making you into the man you are today. She did that through love. It's the only way a person could get the job done so well."

He wanted to tell her how her words soothed the ache that had tormented him ever since he'd read that document. But he didn't know how to say it without sounding like a dweeb who was preoccupied with his innermost feelings. After all, she'd been attracted to the strong, silent cowboy who dug postholes.

Tonight was supposed to be about hearty food, sexy dancing and taking her home to his hand-carved bed. They'd already spent way too long focusing on his identity issues. He'd asked her out to show her a good time, not go into psychoanalysis.

So he angled his head toward the neon sign that depicted a version of Wyoming's logo, a cowboy on a bucking bronc. "Ready for some beef and beer?"

Apparently she was ready to let the loaded subject of his parentage drop, too. "Lead on, cowboy."

As he helped her out of the truck, he allowed himself the pleasure of caressing the bare skin at the small of her back. He'd have fun trying to teach her to dance. He'd have an excuse to touch her all night long.

<u>13</u>

ONCE SHE FELT THE WARMTH of Nick's hand at the small of her back, Dominique regretted lecturing him. She needed to keep her big mouth shut and concentrate on the sexual chemistry between them. What happened with Sarah and his brothers as they worked through this issue was none of her damned business—but she couldn't seem to remember that in the heat of the moment.

Before Nick opened the battered wooden door of the Spirits and Spurs, she heard the wail of a steel guitar. Then he ushered her inside and she tried to absorb the bevy of sights and sounds coming at her. Most of the tables grouped around the dance floor were occupied, but she spied one in the corner that was empty. A polished wooden bar occupied the far right wall.

The band on the small stage consisted of four guys who barely fit up there. The lead singer played an acoustic guitar, and his backup boys were on a slap bass, a banjo and the steel guitar she'd first heard. She couldn't claim to know much about country music, but for a hole-in-the-wall in the middle of nowhere, they sounded darned good.

Couples whirled and stomped on the cozy dance floor. One look at the precision movements and the small space convinced Dominique she didn't want to go there. She didn't relish getting run over or looking like a complete fool. Instead of dancing with Nick, she'd play footsie under the table.

A waitress, down-home cute and dressed in a short flounced skirt and a tight T-shirt with the bar logo in spangles over her breasts, came up immediately. "Want a table, Nick?"

"That'd be great, Carolyn. This is my friend Dominique from Indiana."

"Nice to meet you."

Although the waitress smiled, Dominique felt as if she'd been shoved under a microscope. Nick was probably one of the most eligible bachelors in town, and single girls might not be thrilled that he was escorting a tourist. Dominique had the urge to pin on a sign that read I'll Be Gone in Four Days.

Oh, well. She *would* be gone in four days, whether the local female population knew it or not, and once she'd left the area, the women could go back to pursuing Nick to their heart's content.

After Carolyn showed them to a table and handed them menus, Dominique hid behind hers and leaned over to murmur a comment in Nick's ear. Along the way she noticed he smelled delicious, even better than the aroma of food wafting from the kitchen. "Is there anyone in here tonight you've dated? Because I don't feel exactly welcome."

"Jack's worked me so hard lately I haven't felt much like dating, so the answer is no. Last night was my first time here in months, and I took a few turns around the dance floor with some of the ladies. It's possible they're not overjoyed to see me with someone."

Dominique continued to hide behind her menu. "I'm really hungry, so I want to order some food, but I think it would be torturing these women to drag this out much longer than dinner. We should just eat and leave."

His breath was warm and sweet on her face. "You're chickening out on the dancing, aren't you?"

Reaching under the table, she stroked his thigh. "Aren't there things you'd rather do than dance?"

He caught her hand and held it tight against his denim-clad leg. "You bet. But this isn't about me. It's about you enjoying the complete Wyoming experience. You have to dance."

She spoke through clenched teeth. "But I don't want to dance."

"I know, which is all the more reason. Listen, you're fond of telling me to keep an open mind. Why don't you keep an open mind about dancing with me?"

"Because those cowgirls would as soon trip me on the floor as look at me. I have no experience with contact sports."

He drew her hand up to his crotch, which had a serious bulge going on. "I beg to differ."

She turned her head to look at him behind the screen created by their raised menus. "You're making my case for me. Let's eat quickly and get back to the ranch. Why waste time with silly dancing?"

"Because it'll be fun, and it'll build the suspense."

She rubbed her hand over the warm denim covering his package. "How much suspense can you stand, cowboy?"

"You might be sur—" He stopped talking as Carolyn came over to their table with an order pad.

"You were *such* fun last night, Nick," the waitress said. Then she turned to Dominique. "You should see this man out on the floor. I hope you're prepared to dance, because this guy was made for the two-step."

Dominique would have loved to tell this Carolyn person that she had no intention of giving in to peer pressure and dancing with Nick tonight. But that would only confirm to Carolyn that Dominique didn't belong with Nick and didn't belong in this bar, either.

So instead she put on her best smile and gazed at her. "I've been waiting for a long time to dance the two-step with someone who knows what he's doing. I wouldn't pass this up for anything."

Carolyn eyed her, speculation evident in her intense gaze. There was a liberal dose of doubt in her eyes, but a certain amount of respect, too. "That's great to hear. So what can I get for you two?"

Dominique had pretty much abandoned red meat while she was with Herman, who insisted chicken and fish were the healthier choice. She opened her mouth to order the barbecued chicken, but that wasn't what came out. "I'll have a steak, medium rare, baked potato, loaded, a salad with ranch dressing and a Bud."

"Make that two," Nick said. The minute Carolyn left, he rose from the table. "May I have this dance?"

Oh, Lord, now she'd have to put her money where her mouth was, and this wasn't going to be pretty. But she couldn't back down now. She stood and offered him her hand. "Certainly."

He led her to the dance floor and pulled her in close. "Follow me."

She looked into his eyes. "I am so dead."

"No, you're not." He tightened his grip. "Stay loose and go with my body movements. You'll be fine. It's not that different from sex."

Oh, but it was. As she stumbled around the dance floor in an attempt to follow his cues, she was grateful that sex with him hadn't been this awkward. She and Nick performed much better with their clothes off than on.

Still, it wasn't as bad as she'd feared, and the longer they danced, the better she became at following his rhythm. The guy was a great dancer, and that was kind of a turn-on.

She even became comfortable enough to initiate a little dance floor conversation. "Spirits and Spurs is a clever name for a Western bar. It gets the mention of alcohol in there along with the cowboy reference."

Nick twirled her around, and miracle of miracles, she didn't fall down. "The name has nothing to do with alcohol. At least not primarily."

"But—" She stepped on his toe. "Sorry."

His wince was barely visible. "No worries."

"Spirits and Spurs. It's obvious what it means."

"Not so much. When Josie bought the bar it was called the Rusty Spur." He twirled her again and this time she didn't step on him. "But Josie's convinced that the place is inhabited by the dear departed souls of all the miners and cowboys who've ever loved this place."

"Really? That's sort of cool."

"You've heard of 'Ghost Riders in the Sky.' The locals call Josie's concept 'Ghost Drinkers in the Bar.'"

Dominique started laughing, which made her stumble, but she didn't bother to apologize because it was his fault for making her laugh. "So she really thinks the place is haunted?"

"Yep."

"What's her evidence?"

"The usual. When she's closing up at night and nobody's around, she claims to hear voices, and laughter, and the clink of glasses. When she sweeps the floor there are cold spots, and as she's putting the chairs on the tables, once in a while she feels resistance, as if someone's trying to keep that chair available instead of letting her turn it upside down."

Dominique spoke before she thought. "Did your dad come in here often?"

Nick didn't say anything at first and she thought he'd ignore the question, which would probably be better all the way around. Nick's life was crazy enough without adding in the potential ghost of his dead father.

But then he stopped dancing and gazed at her. "I don't believe in ghosts."

NICK WAS A MAN OF SCIENCE, a medical man. He'd told Dominique the truth—he didn't believe in spirits. Going out to the sacred site to think things through was one thing, a sort of family tradition that he accepted as more like therapy than woo-woo stuff.

Ghosts were a whole other level of strangeness, and logic told him they were the product of someone's over-active imagination. Still, as he guided Dominique back to their table, where their meal waited, he thought about how much he'd love to talk to his father's ghost, if such a ghost existed. Of course it didn't.

But if Jonathan Chance, Sr. had any kind of afterlife presence, it would most likely show up here. He'd been a social guy who'd enjoyed tipping a few with his friends or sharing a meal and two-stepping with Sarah. Sarah had held his sixtieth birthday party here and it had been a blowout.

Nick liked thinking about that party because he couldn't remember a happier family occasion. His dad and Sarah had dominated the dance floor, and Jack— well, he'd been the life of the party, dancing with every woman in the place, including Sarah's eighty-two-year-old mother, Grandma Judy.

Nick and Gabe had watched their older brother in awe as he charmed what seemed like the entire female population of Shoshone that night. What a difference four years had made.

Dominique cleared her throat. "Nick, I apologize. That was a stupid thing for me to have said."

"About my dad's ghost?" He glanced over at her and realized she'd been sitting quietly, waiting for him to come out of his mental fog. She hadn't touched her food.

"Yes. I put my foot in my mouth and I'm so sorry. I hope I haven't ruined our evening."

Nick grinned at her. "Hey, I really don't believe in ghosts, and I'm the one who should apologize. You stirred up a memory, a really good memory, and I sank right into it, which was rude."

"So you're not upset?"

"Hell, no! I was thinking about my dad's sixtieth birthday party here. It was technically a private event, but Josie didn't bother to close the place to anyone because the whole damn town was invited, anyway. It was great."

"I can tell." She smiled back at him. "You look happy."

"It's good to remember things like that, so thanks for jarring it out of my subconscious." He put his napkin in his lap. "Now dig in, because you'll need your strength."

"For the dancing?"

He winked at her. "Well, that, too, I guess." He cut into his steak and was pleased to find it was tender. Josie might not run a five-star restaurant, but she did okay.

He'd taken his second bite when the front door opened and he casually glanced up to see who'd come in. He almost choked on his food. *His mother.* Then he had to mentally correct himself. Not his mother, his stepmother.

She'd arrived with one of her old friends, Lucy Bledsoe, owner of the Lickity Split ice cream parlor. Lucy had been widowed five years ago, and she'd been a huge support to Sarah since Jonathan died.

Somehow Nick had never expected Sarah and Lucy to show up here, although it made perfect sense. Grandma Judy wouldn't want her daughter hovering over her every minute.

Sarah hadn't seen him. He was sure of that from the way she laughed and talked with Carolyn. Now he wished he'd asked Jack if he'd mentioned anything to Sarah. But he would know the minute she laid eyes on him. She'd never been any good at hiding her feelings.

"Nick, what's wrong?" Dominique put a hand on his arm.

Apparently he wasn't any good at hiding his feelings, either, but he couldn't claim to have inherited that from Sarah. Not anymore. It shouldn't matter, but it did. He felt as if he'd lost both parents, and technically, he had.

He gave Dominique a quick glance before returning his attention to the two women. "It's my...it's Sarah. She just came in with her friend Lucy."

"Oh." Dominique's fingers tightened on his arm. "Which one is Sarah?"

"The one with the white hair. Lucy's the redhead."

"My goodness, Sarah's beautiful. Not every woman can get away with letting her hair go white, but she has the cheekbones for it."

"So does her mom. Grandma Judy modeled for some big-deal agency in New York, made piles of money and bought a place out here. She married Grandpa Bill and had Sarah, but didn't want more than one kid, so she'd keep her figure."

"Sarah hasn't spotted you yet."

"Nope. She—okay, Carolyn just told her. They're coming over."

"Look, if you want to talk to her privately, I can suggest to Lucy that we take a seat at the bar."

"Nothing doing." Nick studied Sarah's expression as the two women wound their way through the tables. Her smile was open and welcoming. Jack hadn't said anything.

Nick wasn't sure whether to be relieved or not. Now he had to decide how to play this. If he didn't want to discuss it, he'd have to keep her busy enough that she wouldn't notice anything strange about his behavior.

Smiling, he rose from the table and went forward to meet the women. "Hi, you two! What a great surprise." He deliberately avoided calling Sarah anything. She'd be crushed if he stopped calling her Mom, and yet he didn't know if he'd be able to now without thinking about this whole mess.

"I wish we'd known you'd be here." Sarah gave him a hug and a kiss on the cheek. "We would have come over sooner!"

"It was sort of last-minute." Damned if he didn't breathe in her familiar perfume, a flowery scent his dad had liked, and get a lump in his throat. He was back to being five years old and needing his mom to make everything all right again. Except she was part of the problem.

Lucy followed up with a hug and kiss, too. "It's good

to see you, Nick. I keep thinking you'll come in for a scoop of your favorite chocolate chip cookie dough."

"Jack's keeping us on track out there. Come on, let me introduce you to Dominique." He turned back to the table and discovered she'd left her chair and walked around to meet them. "Dominique Jeffries, I'd like you to meet Sarah Chance and Lucy Bledsoe."

Sarah put her arm around his waist and gave him another hug. "Also known as your *mother*. Sheesh, Nick. You make me sound like a stranger. Very nice to meet you, Dominique. Are you here on business or pleasure?"

"Strictly pleasure." Dominique shook hands with the women. "I'm staying at the ranch. Pam ended up with an overflow situation."

Sarah nodded. "It happens now and then, and we're glad to help out."

"The ranch is gorgeous. I love it there."

"Good." Sarah smiled at her. "Then I hope you'll come back. I'm happy to see that Nick is introducing you to our local nightlife."

Dominique made a face. "Poor guy's trying to teach me the two-step, but I've mangled his toes."

Sarah gazed up at Nick. "You boys take after your father. I married him because he could dance."

Carolyn appeared on the fringe of the group. "I have a table in the corner, unless the two of you want to try and squeeze in here with Nick and his date."

"I wouldn't dream of interrupting Nick's date," Sarah said. "We'll sit at the other table."

Nick couldn't imagine how that would work. No

matter where Sarah and Lucy sat, he'd feel on display. "Sit with us," he said. "I haven't talked to you in a few days. You can tell me how Grandma Judy's doing."

Sarah seemed pleased. "If you're sure it's not a horrible imposition…"

Dominique spoke up immediately. "Of course not. I'd love it if you'd sit with us. I've felt sort of cheated because I couldn't meet the mistress of that beautiful ranch house."

Sarah turned to Carolyn. "Then I guess we'll stay right here."

"You bet," the waitress said. "Do you know what you want to eat, or would you like menus?"

"Oh, you know what I want," Sarah said.

"Me, too," Lucy added. "Us old-timers don't need menus anymore."

Nick volunteered to get a couple of chairs. He was still wrestling with how he wanted to handle this encounter when the band struck up a waltz, and inspiration hit.

After he'd maneuvered the extra chairs around the small table, he held out his hand to Sarah before she'd had a chance to sit down. "I'll bet it's been awhile since you waltzed."

Pure joy filled her blue eyes. "Nick, are you asking me to dance?"

As he met her happy gaze, all his anger melted away. She'd meant no harm. She'd even tried to talk her stubborn husband out of keeping his secret, but in the end she'd given in to his wishes because she'd loved him. "Yes, Mom, I am, if you'll do me the honor."

14

DOMINIQUE LONGED TO BE a mouse in Nick's pocket, so she could listen in on the conversation they were having on the dance floor.

"Those Chance men are dancers, every last one of them," Lucy said. "It's good to see Nick out there. The man has great buns, doesn't he?"

Dominique laughed. "Yes. Yes, he does." Although dancing with Nick meant being held close and feeling his animal magnetism, watching him dance brought its own kind of sensual delight. He really was a gorgeous man.

And when he had a partner who could dance, the two of them were poetry in motion. If Dominique were going to hang around—which she wasn't—she'd have to learn. Herman, who had no rhythm, had lulled her into thinking the skill wasn't important.

But when it meant sweeping around the floor with a man like Nick, it became important. Dominique envied Sarah her grace and style. She was wearing jeans, but from the way she moved, Dominique could imagine her in a ball gown.

Love glowed in her expression as she gazed up at Nick. Dominique had no doubt Sarah loved him as her son, even if she hadn't physically given birth to him. Apparently Nick had no doubt of that love, either. When he'd called her "Mom," Dominique's heart had squeezed.

She doubted they were discussing the document Nick had found. He'd apparently decided against confrontation and in favor of bonding with this woman who had raised him. Dominique loved watching them together. A man who showed that kind of empathy toward his mother would make somebody a terrific husband.

Too bad she wasn't in the market for a boyfriend, let alone a permanent life partner. After two years with Herman, she knew what she *didn't* want, but she was still working out what she did. For starters, he'd need to live in Indiana. Maybe she should consider Nick an example of the kind of man she'd look for eventually.

Carolyn arrived with two glasses and two bottles of beer. She placed one of each in front of Lucy and at the empty place where Sarah would sit. "I'll be right back with your food." She whisked away again.

"Thanks, Carolyn," Lucy called after her. Ignoring the glass, she picked up her beer and drank. "My husband was a cowboy, and this is how I learned to drink beer, straight from the bottle. A cowboy can't be bothered with glasses. Too much trouble."

Dominique forced herself to stop watching Nick

dance so she could politely pay attention to Lucy. "Have you lived in this area long?"

"Forty-five years. Came here from Missouri as a young bride. Very young bride. Barely twenty." She took another swig from her beer.

"That's young."

"Young and foolish. Tom showed up for a wedding of one of my cousins and I fell in love. I agreed to marry him and move to a place I'd never seen, with a man I barely knew." She gazed at Dominique. "Sometimes it pays to be foolish. I still thank God I didn't do the sensible thing and stay in Missouri."

"But how does a person know when to be foolish and when to play it safe?"

"Excellent question. I have a couple of kids, one on the East Coast and one on the West Coast. They pretty much asked the same thing, so I'll tell you what I told them. Listen to your heart."

Dominique groaned. "Lucy, people are always saying that, but what does it mean?"

"Exactly what it says, dear."

"But when I'm thinking of doing something, I have all these competing voices in my head. I'd need a traffic controller to sort them out. How can I tell which of those voices is coming from my heart?"

"For one thing, you should actually feel warmth in your chest. The heart registers emotion, you know. That's not just a myth. So check that out."

Dominique automatically looked over at the dance floor where Nick was finishing the waltz with a dramatic dip. Sarah was laughing.

"Feel some warmth?" Lucy asked.

"This isn't about Nick," Dominique said quickly. "It's about what I want to do with my life."

"The right man could be part of that decision."

"True, but I think a woman needs to know what she wants before she takes on a commitment to a guy. Right now I'm confused about that."

"There's a big rock located on the Last Chance that's sacred to the Shoshone tribe. Sarah took me out there when Tom died. That's where I got the idea to open my ice cream parlor."

"I've heard of that site." Dominique wasn't about to tell Lucy what had happened there last night.

"Get Nick to show you where it is. You might find some answers."

Dominique nodded. "Good suggestion. Thanks."

Lucy held a hand over her chest. "But if you get really warm here, it's your heart saying that what you're considering might sound foolish to others, but it's perfect for you."

Carolyn came over carrying two platters, each containing a steak and a baked potato. She balanced two bowls of salad on her forearm. "One Lucy special and one Sarah special." She put everything on the table. "How are we doing on drinks?"

"Bring us another round," Lucy said. "This is turning into a party."

Dominique grinned. "I do believe it is." She handed Carolyn her glass. "And you can take this. From now on, I'm drinking straight from the bottle."

NICK CUT HIMSELF OFF after two beers because he was driving, but he enjoyed watching his mother, Lucy and Dominique get mildly plastered. The two older women would walk home, and Dominique would be riding with him.

He worked off some of the beer dancing with each of the women in turn. Lucy got such a kick out of doing the two-step that he was sorry he hadn't asked her before. As for Dominique, the beer seemed to loosen her up and improve her rhythm.

His mother obviously was having more fun than she'd had since his father died. Only a cruel person would have spoiled the evening by bringing up a complicated issue like the true story of his birth. Nick didn't have it in him to be cruel.

He debated whether he ever had to bring it up. If Nick let it drop, so would Jack, who was fiercely protective of Sarah. Gabe wouldn't have to know, either. Jack had certainly proved he could keep a secret, and Nick couldn't see the advantage in blabbing it to Gabe.

Maybe none of that ancient history mattered, anyway. Nick had been raised with people who had loved him and cared for him. Digging up the past wouldn't do anybody any good.

Or so he tried to tell himself as he and Dominique walked Lucy back to her apartment behind the ice cream shop and his mom to Grandma Judy's.

"She'll be asleep now," his mother said as they hugged goodbye at the door to his grandmother's little cottage, "or I'd invite you in to see her. I know Jack's turned into a slave driver, but tell him you need an afternoon off to come in and see Grandma. Better yet, make him come with you."

"I'll do that."

"And I'm so glad to meet you, Dominique." His mother gave Dominique a goodbye hug, too.

Nick stood to one side and watched the two women as they took their leave of each other. They would get along if given the opportunity to become friends, not that it mattered. Tonight had been a moment in time he'd always remember, but quite likely it was an isolated event never to be repeated.

He took Dominique's hand as they returned to the parking lot at the Spirits and Spurs. Shoshone had never known the luxury of sidewalks, so they walked on the edge of the asphalt. In a town this small he didn't worry about being run over.

He gave her hand a squeeze. "Thanks for being so gracious to my mom and her friend."

"It was easy. Lucy's a kick and I really like your mom."

"Good. So do I."

"Are you ever going to tell her?"

"I've been thinking about that." He found it interesting that Dominique had latched on to the very thing he'd been turning over in his mind. They'd done that with each other more times than not. He wondered if it meant anything.

"And what did you decide?" She laced her fingers more securely through his, as if she enjoyed the contact.

He sure as hell did. Holding hands had never seemed

like a big deal once he'd graduated from high school, but with Dominique, it seemed huge. Maybe that was because of the way they'd started, bypassing the preliminaries and going straight for the sex. Now the little things—holding hands, helping her with her chair— were more significant because those courtesies weren't just to woo her into bed.

"For one thing," he said, "my brother Jack can keep a secret like nobody's business. He's kept this one for almost thirty years. Same goes for Mary Lou and Emmett. If I say nothing more about it, this whole issue can disappear."

"I guess you're right. What about Gabe, though?"

"I suppose I wouldn't have to tell him, either." Nick realized his younger brother hadn't ever called him back. That wasn't like Gabe, but maybe he'd had to wait until tonight. Nick had left his cell phone at home because he hadn't wanted anything to interrupt his evening with Dominique.

"Could you really keep it from Gabe?"

"Maybe. I think so. And tonight, when we were all having such a good time, I thought that's the way it should be." He glanced both ways before walking with her across the street. As usual, nobody was coming.

"And now?"

"Now that some of the euphoria has worn off, I have to admit there's a problem with letting it all go. Or I should say *I* have a problem with letting it go."

Pulling the keys from his pocket, he unlocked the truck. "I want to know who I am, who I come from. Sarah's great, but she didn't give birth to me. I want to know something about the woman who did. All I have is a name, and it's not enough."

Dominique nodded. "I get that."

"You do?" He couldn't believe the relief flooding through him. She was the only person he could talk with, and having her understanding was huge. "You don't think that's the most selfish idea you've ever heard?"

"Of course not. You're not a mystery baby with no traceable past. Someday you may have your own children, and you'll want to know as much about your background as possible, both so you can tell them and because medically it's always a good idea to know something about your parents."

"Exactly. I assume she died, but I don't know how or why."

"Sarah probably knows something and she might give you leads to find out more. Now that I've met her, I'm sure she'd want to help you. She adores you, Nick."

"And I adore her. You were right that she loves me like a son, no matter whether she gave birth to me or not. I'd become so wrapped up in my righteous indignation that I'd forgotten how precious that love is. When I asked her to dance…" He didn't go on, afraid he'd choke up if he tried to explain the way he'd felt at that moment.

Dominique moved in close and slipped a warm hand under his shirt collar to cup the back of his neck. She lifted her face to his. "That was one of the sweetest things I've ever seen, when you held out your hand to her."

He reached up to cradle her head. "*You're* the sweetest

thing I've ever seen. I hope you don't mind public displays of affection, because I'm about to make one."

"It's not very public," she murmured. "Nobody's here but us."

He lowered his head, almost touching her mouth. "But anyone could come along, and they'd see me kiss you. We've never kissed in public before."

"Worried about my reputation?"

He smiled. "No, mine." But he kissed her anyway, because he couldn't help it. He'd hungered for a real kiss ever since that quick brush of lips they'd shared before they'd left the house tonight.

He couldn't be satisfied by a wimpy kiss at this point in the action, even though they were standing under the dusk-to-dawn light that illuminated the bar's parking lot, which was only a few yards from the town's only major intersection. He might as well put up a neon sign announcing that he was involved with Dominique Jeffries, the photographer from Indianapolis.

And he was involved. The moment he settled into the kiss, he realized just how much. He relished the taste of her, the velvet pressure of her mouth, the teasing movement of her tongue. Kissing Dominique was like coming home.

No other woman had made him feel like that. That should frighten him, because Dominique was probably going to break his heart. If he had any sense he wouldn't continue down this dead-end road.

But when she was in his arms, he forgot everything but the present. He knew she would leave in a few days, but she was here now. He could hold her close and savor the way her body rose to meet his, the way she fit so neatly against him, the way his cock swelled in anticipation of what they'd do once they left this parking lot.

Someone drove past and let out a long wolf whistle. Although Nick didn't care who saw him kissing Dominique, or how the gossip mill would interpret it, he couldn't continue with this seduction in the middle of the Spirits and Spurs parking lot. He wouldn't say public nudity never happened within the town limits, but there was an ordinance against it.

Lifting his head, he gazed down at her flushed face. Even in the harsh light from the overhead lamp she was beautiful. But she would be even more beautiful lying naked in his hand-carved bed. "Ready for a more private venue?"

"Are you actually suggesting that we go retro and find a bed?"

"I am." And the longer he stood there holding her, the more immediate his need for that horizontal surface became.

She rubbed her hands up and down his back. "What a novel idea."

"It's an idea whose time has come." Wrapping an arm around her waist, he walked her to the passenger side of the truck, unlocked the door and helped her in. "Let's go home."

15

DOMINIQUE HADN'T MISSED his "Let's go home," a comment that could have been an offhand one, but she didn't think so. For a man like Nick, a man with a heart the size of the whole Teton Range, that statement would have significance.

The comment itself wasn't nearly as worrisome as her reaction to it. She'd loved hearing him say that, loved listening to his soft baritone resonating with his anticipated pleasure. She wrapped herself in that warmth and allowed his suggestion to run in a continuous loop through her mind as he drove down the dark road toward the ranch.

She wasn't surprised when he switched on the truck's radio so they were serenaded with country tunes on the way back. The music maintained the happy mood they'd established at the bar. She also wasn't surprised when he reached over and took her hand.

Foolish or not, they were falling for each other. She couldn't deny that her heart had melted when she'd watched him dancing with his mother. But that was only the final item on a list that had grown with each moment they'd spent together. First she'd been impressed with his care and compassion in the meadow. Sure, she'd also been impressed with his body, but his kindness hadn't escaped her notice, either.

Later on she'd met the two adorable dogs he'd rescued, and that night she'd seen him at his most vulnerable, when he'd discovered the truth about his parentage. They'd bonded over that, whether they'd meant to or not.

She'd also seen his playful side. The image of him leaving her room wearing a towel and clenching a cigar between his teeth would stay with her forever. A woman would have to be made of stone not to succumb to the charms of Nick Chance.

Add to that his obvious interest in her, and she had a recipe for disaster. They needed time to discover if this was a relationship that would last, but they were running out of it. If she ripped up her life on the basis of an affair of a few short days, no matter how charming the guy, everyone she knew would figure she was back to her old flaky self.

They would be right. Giving up a successful business and trying to start over in a new town that was part of a highly competitive market was financial insanity. Even Dominique, who tended to ignore the bottom line, could see that.

Nick glanced at her. "You're very quiet over there."

"I'm thinking."

"That's a bad sign."

She turned toward him. She adored that strong

profile, loved kissing those firm lips. "You know what's happening."

He met her gaze briefly. "Yeah. I've been fighting it from the first time I saw you, but I don't seem to be winning that fight."

"Me, either."

He rubbed his thumb over the back of her hand. "Good to know I'm not in this mess alone."

"Not by a long shot."

He took a deep breath. "I want you to stick around, Dominique, and I know how ridiculous that sounds. I know you can't just set up shop here in Shoshone, or even Jackson, and be sure you'd earn a living. You've built a successful business back home, and you'd be crazy to abandon that just because I can't stand for you to leave."

"My mother suggested I should try to get the ranch to hire me to take pictures of your horses for the Web site. Mind you, she wasn't imagining I'd move out here. She only wanted me to open up a new avenue of business."

"In that respect, it's a good idea. But that alone wouldn't support you if you moved here. Not even close."

Dominique decided she might as well lay out every possibility, to make sure she wasn't missing anything. "She thought I could interest people in having a profes-sional photograph of the horse they bought. You know, to hang up somewhere."

"Maybe, and I'm not saying they wouldn't, but—"

"Nick, I'm embarrassed to be throwing out these ideas, but I thought I should at least mention it."

"Definitely. But I've watched this process a lot over the years, and people who have just bought an expensive animal are usually recovering from sticker shock. They might not be willing to shell out another dime. Some might, but it's—"

"Grasping at straws. I know."

"At least you're trying to find an answer, and all I am is a wet blanket." He sighed. "I want like hell to say you could survive as a photographer out here, but I don't know that you would."

"So we should both consider this a nice interlude and let it go at that."

"Goddammit." His grip on her hand tightened. "That isn't working for me, Dominique."

"For me, either." Rash thoughts ran through her mind. If she couldn't make money as a photographer, she'd do something else. She'd apply for a job at the Lickity Split or the Spirits and Spurs. She'd waited tables before. She could wait tables again if it meant being with Nick.

Then she caught herself. What was she doing? Photography was her calling, and to abandon the business she'd painstakingly built because she'd fallen for a guy was the sort of thing she would have done a few years ago. How discouraging to think she'd been on the brink of doing it again.

She took a deep breath. "This is why I said we shouldn't get involved in the first place, remember?"

"Who could have predicted we'd be so perfect for each other?"

"Pam. When I talked with her that first day, she told me I was your type. She said you wouldn't be able to have a no-strings-attached affair with me, and she was right on the money. But we both charged ahead anyway."

"Yeah." Nick was silent for the rest of the drive home, but he didn't let go of her hand.

As he pulled the truck into the circular drive and switched off the engine, she gazed at him, her heart aching. "Let's cut our losses. I'll see about changing my ticket so I can fly out tomorrow. If I can't, I'll move back to Pam's until I can get a flight."

His jaw tightened. "It's probably a good idea."

"It's a terrible idea, but I don't have a better one."

"You could always stay here rent free, and maybe help Mary Lou or something while you tried to get your photography business going."

"Our relationship is still in the baby stages. I could change my whole life around for nothing."

He cleared his throat, as if he might want to argue that point, but after a brief hesitation, all he said was, "Right."

"Besides, my financial independence has been a long time coming. I spent too many years living hand-to-mouth, but thanks to a dose of reality and Herman's guidance, I have a thriving business. I'd be foolish to give it up for something that may or may not work out."

"Yes, you would." Nick squeezed her hand and released it. "Guess that's it, then." He reached for his door handle.

She reached for hers, too. Later she might cry, but for now she just needed to get out of the truck and away from Nick before she weakened. She was making the right decision. She needed to see it through.

"Stay there and I'll help you down."

"I'm perfectly capable of—"

"I know you are! It's a courtesy, a way of showing that I respect you and…oh, never mind." He climbed out of the truck.

So did she, and found him waiting for her. She glanced up into his shadowed face. "This is my fault. If I hadn't walked out into that meadow and taken your picture, then none of this would have happened."

"But then I would have missed some of the most wonderful moments of my life."

Her breath caught. "You don't regret any of this?"

"Not a single second."

Swamped by an emotion she dared not voice, she swallowed the lump in her throat. "Me, either."

"You can't go anywhere until tomorrow."

Her battered heart kicked into a faster rhythm. "I know, but it would be easier if we—"

"Are you kidding?" His laugh was low and rich with desire. "I can't speak for you, but I won't sleep a wink knowing you're right down the hall and you'll be gone in the morning."

What he was suggesting made no sense at all. They were trying to disengage from each other, not entangle themselves even more. And yet, he was right. She wouldn't sleep, either.

There was plenty of air to be had out here under the stars, but she couldn't seem to draw much of it into her lungs. "I suppose…" She stopped, and then rushed the last part. "If neither of us will be sleeping, we might as well keep each other company."

"I was hoping you'd say that." Taking her hand, he led her up the porch steps and into the house.

Although his touch literally made her knees weak, she managed to climb the stairs and walk down the dark hallway without making him carry her. No doubt he would have—could have—but she wanted him to save his strength. They bypassed her room and stepped into his, where he'd left a light burning.

His bed was gorgeous. The headboard depicted a forest scene of two wolves baying at a full moon. But when she noticed that the covers were turned back and a single rose lay against the snowy sheets, she nearly lost it. "Oh, Nick. I would have missed this."

He drew her into his arms. "And I would have missed this." His lips found hers in the sweetest, most gentle kiss they'd ever shared.

Tears threatened to fall, but she squeezed her eyes shut to hold them at bay. She wouldn't cry tonight. Tonight she would make love with Nick.

They undressed each other slowly, pausing to touch, to kiss, to murmur words of appreciation. Up to now, Nick had given her the best sex of her life. But tonight was about more than sex, and he seemed to realize it, too.

When at last he urged her down to the cool sheets, he framed her face in both hands. His green eyes glowed with purpose. "I will never forget making love to you."

"I won't forget making love to you, either."

He gave her a slow, sensuous smile. "That's why I wanted you here, so I could make sure of that. Everything else was fun, but I do my best work on a bed."

Anticipation surged through her, leaving her achy and wet. "I don't know, Nick. We've had some spectacular sex."

"Yeah." He leaned down to trace her lips with his tongue. "But this is the time you'll remember."

She understood what he meant. With fingertips, mouth and tongue he explored every inch of her body. By the time he reached her toes, she was writhing on the bed, so hot from wanting him that she was whimpering.

But he wasn't finished. Rolling her over, he kissed her nape, her shoulders, the curve of her spine, the small of her back, the backs of her knees. He licked her bare bottom, and before she quite realized what he had in mind, he turned over on his back and scooted up between her thighs. He urged her to lift her hips.

Crazed with lust, she complied, and then sank down against his waiting mouth. Shamelessly, she took the climax that he seemed so eager to give her. She longed to scream at the top of her lungs, but others shared this house, so she buried her cries in the pillow as he made her come, his strong hands holding her tight.

By the time he rolled her to her back, she was gasping for breath and still vibrating with the force of her orgasm. The snap of latex barely registered, but when she felt him, full and hard, moving into her, she knew he was ready to take his pleasure at last.

"Open your eyes," he murmured.

Sliding both hands up his muscled chest slick with sweat, she lifted her gaze to his.

"Pam was right." He eased his cock into her with steady deliberation. "You're my dream girl."

"No." She rebelled at the hopelessness of that statement. "I can't be."

"Sure you can." He completed the connection, settling against her with a sigh. "A guy doesn't always end up with his dream girl."

"I want you to be happy."

"I'm happy now." He drew back and pushed home again. "That has to be enough."

"If only—"

"Shh." He leaned down and nibbled at her lips. "No regrets. I feel your arms around me, your legs around me, and I'll never forget being cradled by your body. I'll never forget the sensation of my cock sliding into you. Warm… Wet…"

Another orgasm hovered near, fueled by his touch and his erotic voice. "This is good, Nick."

"You bet it is." He began to pump faster. "It's the best, Dominique. No, don't close your eyes. I want to watch you come."

She locked her gaze with his as the pressure mounted. They'd been lovers such a short time, and yet he knew her, knew what she needed to send her over the edge. And he gave it to her, stroking until she lifted to meet his thrusts.

"That's it." The heat in his eyes urged her onward. "Now, my love. *Now.*"

They rocketed upward together, arching across the

night sky. And as she drifted back to earth, his words caught her, easing her descent. *My love.*

THE NIGHT HAD BEEN HEAVEN, but the morning was hell. Nick stumbled through it with as much grace as he could manage. Dominique had returned to her room before dawn. As if by mutual agreement, they said nothing to each other when she slipped out.

He dressed quickly and headed for the barn, where Butch and Sundance were more than glad to see him. He played around with the dogs for a while before heading into the barn to work. Better not to watch Dominique leave. Yet, as Fate would have it, he looked out the door just as Pam was loading Dominique's suitcase into the Bunk and Grub Jeep.

A moment later, Dominique came out and climbed into the passenger seat. She glanced over at the barn, and he ducked back into the shadows, reluctant to let her see him gazing after her like a lovesick fool. Which he was.

But this was as it should be. He felt no ambivalence as he used the time-honored therapy of mucking stalls to work through his angst. The dogs looked on with a soulful doggy gaze, as if they knew he was in pain. He'd live with that pain as long as necessary. He loved her, and because he loved her, he had to let her go.

When Pam's Jeep pulled out of the drive, he refused to watch it leave. Instead he kept shoveling. He would always be grateful for what they'd had together. Nothing could take that away.

"Did I see Dominique leaving with Pam just now?"

Glancing up, Nick discovered Emmett standing in a shaft of sunlight coming through the barn door. The dogs jumped up to greet him.

Nick dumped another load of straw into the wheelbarrow. "She's headed back to Indianapolis."

"That seems kind of sudden." Emmett scrubbed a hand over each of the dogs in turn.

"It's for the best."

"Want to talk about it?"

"No." Nick leaned on his shovel and studied Emmett. The guy was acting natural as he stood there petting the dogs, so he probably hadn't talked to Jack about Nick yet. "How was your picnic?"

Emmett looked away. "I think maybe I'm too old to get started with the picnic thing."

"Want to talk about it?"

"No." Emmett adjusted the tilt of his brown Stetson. "But I think you have the right idea. I'll grab me a shovel."

"Emmett, wait."

The foreman paused, his bushy eyebrows lifted. "What's up?"

"What can you tell me about Nicole O'Leary?"

Emmett stiffened. "Who?"

"Nicole. My mother."

Emmett stared at him. "How in the *hell* did you find out about that?"

"Remember when Jack told me to go through that old trunk of Dad's?"

"Oh, Jesus. I didn't even consider…"

"Neither did Jack. I found the document from when I

was born, the one where she said if anything happened to her, I was to be sent here to be raised by my father." Nick was surprised that he didn't feel the usual sharp pain when he discussed that piece of paper. Either he was already healing, or that pain had been replaced with a deeper one involving Dominique.

Emmett ran a hand over his face. "I'm sorry, son. I wondered if this day would ever come. I told Jonathan he should... But that's not important now. Who knows you found it?"

"Jack. Well, and Dominique. She walked into the office right after I'd pulled it out of the trunk."

"Surely that's not why she's leaving?"

"No. That situation is...complicated. So did you ever meet Nicole?"

Emmett gestured toward a couple of old wooden chairs over by the barn door. "Have a seat."

Leaning his shovel against the back wall, Nick walked out of the stall and over to one of the chairs. The dogs followed and plopped on the floor, one next to each chair.

Emmett broke off a piece of straw from a nearby hay bale and stuck it between his teeth. "It's times like this I wish I hadn't given up my chaw."

"It's times like this I wish I'd started chewing."

"Don't take it up, son. It's a nasty habit." Emmett gazed straight ahead. "So you want to know about Nicole."

"Yeah. And don't sanitize it, Emmett."

The straw wiggled in the corner of Emmett's mouth as he chewed it slowly. "All right. She was one of those free-love people. Do whatever feels good and don't worry about the consequences. She was an artist, but I doubt she ever made much money on her paintings. Jonathan and I got the impression her folks were rich and they supported her."

Nick could see some parallels with Dominique, but there were some glaring differences, too. Dominique had tried to avoid getting tangled up with him. Plus she was fiercely independent and determined to hang on to the business she'd built.

"So you did actually know her, then?"

"Oh, yeah. I was at the bar—back when it was called the Rusty Spur—with your dad when Nicole breezed in. She was a knockout—long dark hair, green eyes, great figure." Emmett glanced at him. "You have her eyes."

"And that explains so much. Nobody else in the family has green eyes. When I used to ask Mom, I mean Sarah, she'd—"

"She's still your mother." Emmett's voice had an edge to it. "I don't want you ever throwing this up to her, and if you take after your idiot big brother and start calling her Sarah now because she's not your biological mother, I'll whip your butt. And don't think I can't."

Nick smiled. "I know you can. Don't worry. Sarah is my mom in all the ways that count. She only kept the secret because she loved my dad so much. I get that." And he had Dominique to thank for helping him see it.

"Good thing you do. You gotta understand how it was. Here was your dad, divorced and lonely, depressed. Letting his folks do most of the raising of little Jack.

Then Nicole shows up. He knew she wasn't going to stick around, but he enjoyed her while she was here. I guess they got careless, but neither of them realized they'd created you before she took off again."

"So I really was a total surprise to him." The document had said as much, but Nick felt better hearing it again from Emmett.

"A total surprise to him and to his new wife, Sarah, who was already pregnant with Gabe. Along comes this five-month-old baby delivered in a taxi by a lawyer, a baby conceived during an affair your dad had more than a year ago, before he'd even started courting Sarah."

Nick could picture the shock of that. "My dad never did like admitting his mistakes."

"Nooo, he surely didn't. You were the talk of the town for a while, but he convinced everyone it would be better to raise you thinking Sarah was your mother. As time went by, some who knew the truth moved or passed on, and others forgot it."

Nick contemplated that for a while. "He must have thought if I ever found out, I'd pass judgment on him."

"Probably." Emmett chewed on his straw. "He was always pretty hard on himself, so he must have figured you'd be hard on him, too."

Nick sighed. "Jack has a lot of Dad in him."

"That he does, son. That he does."

"So what happened to Nicole?"

"According to the lawyer who delivered you, she went skydiving. Chute never opened."

Nick winced.

"Yeah, I'm sure your dad had the same reaction. If

you ask me, it was a dumb thing for a new mother to do, but she wasn't that sensible in the first place."

"You didn't like her."

"A person couldn't dislike Nicole. She was a lot of fun. But she was young and immature." Emmett glanced at him. "You said Jack knew you'd found out. What about your mother?"

"I'll talk with her soon."

"And Gabe?"

"Soon."

"Don't let it go too long, Nick. Gabe has a thing about being treated like the baby of the family. He wouldn't like it if he thought you were trying to protect him from this news."

"You're right." Nick stood. "I'll go call him again. That is, if you don't mind finishing up that stall."

"Glad to do it." Emmett rose from his chair and rested his hand on Nick's shoulder. "No one meant any harm, son."

"I know, Emmett. I know."

Emmett gave his shoulder a squeeze. "Go call your brother."

"Right."

Back in his room, Nick steeled himself against the lingering scent of Dominique's perfume, grabbed his cell phone from the dresser and took it downstairs. Once there, he flopped into one of the big leather armchairs.

Before he could dial Gabe's number, he noticed that he had a text message. Sitting up straight, he checked it eagerly, forgetting that Dominique didn't have his number. She'd never needed it.

The message from Gabe had been left the night before, while Nick was at the Spirits and Spurs.

Glad birth went okay. Headed home for a bit. Bringing Top Drawer and Finicky, plus mare. She foundered, was going to auction if I didn't step in. Paid way too much. Jack will probably hit roof. Driving straight through. See you tomorrow.

Nick thought Jack probably would hit the roof. When a horse foundered, the anklebone protruded through the hoof, the same condition that had killed the great racehorse Barbaro. But Gabe had a little of the savior in him, too.

And now Nick could tell him the big news in person.

16

DOMINIQUE'S FLIGHT DIDN'T leave until afternoon, but she wanted out of Shoshone ASAP, so she'd talked Pam into driving her to Jackson right away. She'd rather sit in the relative anonymity of the airport than hang around the Bunk and Grub.

"I'm sorry things worked out this way," Pam said as they neared the outskirts of Jackson.

"I should have listened to you. Nick got attached. Hell, *I* got attached. But you're a successful businesswoman. Would you throw away everything you've worked for on the slight chance something will materialize with a guy?"

Pam's laugh had a tinge of sadness. "Funny you should ask. No, I wouldn't, but it appears my success is a stumbling block to romance for me, too."

"With Emmett?"

"Mmm."

"In what way?"

Her expression tense, Pam tapped her finger against the steering wheel. Obviously the subject frustrated her.

"Emmett doesn't have a lot of money, mostly because it isn't important to him."

"I can see that. He lives on the ranch, doesn't seem to own much of anything. Was he ever married?"

"Yes, almost thirty years ago. It didn't last long, but he has a daughter. He paid child support until she was of age, but he's continued to subsidize whatever she wants to do. She tried to make it in Hollywood, and started a couple of home-based businesses that fizzled."

"Sounds like an expensive kid." Dominique had been, too, until she'd become embarrassed about costing her parents so much and had stopped taking what they offered.

Pam shrugged. "It's no big deal. Emmett doesn't need much, so if he wants to indulge his daughter, that's fine with me."

"So what's the problem?"

"He's uncomfortable getting involved with a woman who's so much wealthier than he is."

Dominique groaned. "That's so old school!"

"Emmett *is* old school. Mostly I find that endearing, until it comes between us. He told me flat out yesterday that he really likes me, but we could never be on equal terms because of my bank balance. So he won't let himself be attracted to me."

"I'm sorry, Pam. That's his loss, though. I have to believe eventually he'll figure that out."

"I'm fifty-eight. I'm not as good at biding my time as I used to be. I'd like…things to be different." She glanced over at Dominique. "Is your camera handy?"

"I always keep it handy. Why?"

"Would you indulge me in something?"

"If you want me to take your picture, I'd be delighted. Just pick a spot."

"Nope, that's not it." She pulled into a parking space in front of one of Jackson's many art galleries. "I'm sure you have Last Chance Ranch pictures in your camera. I want you to show them to my friend Stuart."

Dominique's professional pride caused her to instantly rebel. "They're not edited. Unless he has a compatible cable and computer program, he'll have to look at them on my tiny screen. Nothing looks good that small."

"It won't matter. Stuart has a good eye. Come on." She opened her door.

"Pam, you're not a photographer, so I know you don't understand this, but I would rather have a root canal than show these pictures to another professional until I've cleaned them up, edited them, matted them, made them more—"

"Do you have a plan for hanging on to Nick?" Pam left her door open as she turned toward Dominique, her expression determined.

Dominique blinked. "I'm not hanging on to Nick. I thought you understood that it's just not going to work out."

"I understand there are obstacles, but you didn't build a successful business without learning how to work around obstacles."

"Pam, if you think that I'll take my pictures in there and your friend will go ballistic over them, and then I'll decide I can move here and sell photos to tourists… that's a pipe dream. I'm sure Stuart has a long list of photographers who would love to display their work in his gallery. Their polished, edited, matted and framed work."

"Do you believe in Fate?"

Dominique groaned. "You're killing me here, Pam. The flaky person I used to be would have said yes, of course, and Nick is my soul mate. I would have moved here with no job and no prospects—but I'm not that person anymore."

"I'm not asking you to be that person. I'm asking you to show your *professional* shots to Stuart, because I have an instinctive feeling about you. I've had that feeling ever since you arrived at the Bunk and Grub. If Stuart likes what he sees, great. I'll lay out my plan. If he doesn't like what he sees, then you can fly off into the sunset."

"He won't like what he sees."

"Prove it to me. Bring your camera and come with me."

Dominique figured she'd suffered through more embarrassing things, and anyway, she'd never have to see this Stuart person again. Pam didn't understand how fruitless this was, but she wouldn't be satisfied until Dominique agreed to play along. Hoisting her backpack to her shoulder, Dominique climbed out of the Jeep and followed Pam into the gallery.

Stuart turned out to be a short, balding man who obviously worshipped Pam. Dominique gathered that she had bought a large portion of her wall art from him. From the way he gazed at her, Dominique guessed he had a case of unrequited love. Too bad, but Pam's heart belonged to Emmett.

Of course Stuart agreed to look at the photos. He even produced a cable and transferred the images to his computer screen. When the first pictures of Nick appeared, she felt her cheeks grow warm. She couldn't look at them without remembering what had happened after that.

But another part of her brain, the critical photographer part, was astounded at how good the shots were. Some of her unease over showing them to the gallery owner faded as he clicked through the pictures. She'd meant to gauge his reaction, but instead found herself engrossed by her own work.

When he came to the early morning pictures of a pensive Nick gazing down the road, he paused on one particular shot. "Do you have a release for this?"

"No. I meant to get one, but—"

"I'll get one," Pam said immediately. "I know the subject."

"I could sell the heck out of this picture," Stuart said. "I already know how I'd want to mat and frame it. Some of the others are great, too, but this is the one that's the moneymaker. We'll do very well with it, assuming you get a release from the guy."

"Don't worry about that part," Pam said. "Let's put some paperwork together. This lady has a plane to catch."

Stuart turned to Dominique. "You're not local?"

"No. I have a studio in Indianapolis."

His face fell. "Then I suppose you'll want to sell this

out of your studio. When you came in, I thought you were offering to—"

"I am," Dominique said.

He still looked uncertain. "We like to showcase our photographers, have events where you sign limited editions, things like that. Would you be willing to come back out once in a while?"

Dominique glanced at Pam, who was grinning.

"She'll be happy to do that," she answered for her. "In fact, if she can build a reputation here, she could spend quite a bit of time in Jackson Hole. She's talked about hiring an assistant to handle her studio in Indianapolis."

Dominique's jaw dropped. "Pam! I haven't—"

"Right. You haven't made that public yet. But Stuart needs to know, so he can schedule you for a showing. Any free time this month, Stuart?"

"As Fate would have it, somebody canceled out of an event I had planned for two weekends from now. That should give us enough time to complete the matting and framing. Dominique, if you'll leave it all to me, we'll have something spectacular ready in a couple of weeks. Can you fly back out?"

She felt a little dizzy, but not so dizzy she didn't know the right answer. "Yes. Yes, I can."

"Excellent." He held out his hand. "Congratulations. This is brilliant work. I just know you'll be a huge hit."

Once they were back in the Jeep, Dominique sank against the upholstery and gulped air.

"Told you," Pam said.

Dominique glanced at her. "Okay, that was way more excitement and enthusiasm than I anticipated, but it could still be a bust. Don't be expecting me to go home and hire that assistant yet."

"You could interview a few people."

"You're incorrigible! I will not!"

"For an artistic type, you sure are careful."

"Because I didn't used to be, Pam. I know what it's like to be working a minimum wage job while you try desperately to find time for your art. My crappy boyfriend, much as I hate to give him credit for it, taught me how to be more practical about my career. So I'm not about to jeopardize that while I chase after some pie-in-the-sky dream."

Pam started the Jeep and pulled back into traffic. "All right. So tell me how you want to handle the situation. I have to get the release from Nick. Do you want him to know any of this?"

"No, I don't. Let him think I want it because I'm going to display the pictures in Indianapolis. Let's find out if the show's a success before bringing Nick into it."

"You won't try to see him when you come back in two weeks?"

Dominique hesitated, but she had to be strong. "No. If I crash and burn, I don't want Nick to be there watching it happen. That would be too painful for both of us."

"Stuart will be advertising the exhibit. There's always the possibility Nick will come into Jackson and see a flyer."

"How much of a possibility?"

"Honestly, not much. Nick doesn't come here that often."

"Okay, then. I'll ask you to keep this a secret."

"I can do that, Dominique. Believe me, I'm good at keeping secrets."

GABE'S MUD-SPATTERED truck pulled in late in the afternoon. He'd called ahead, so Nick, Emmett and Jack were waiting for him.

As Gabe climbed down from the cab and took off his gray Stetson to scrub a hand through his dark blond hair, Nick realized how much he looked like Sarah. He had those same chiseled cheekbones and the same blue eyes. Although her hair had turned white in the past ten years, it had been about the color of Gabe's when she was younger.

Emmett, Jack and Nick walked over to greet him. Emmett and Jack shook his hand, but Nick hugged him, because they'd always had that kind of relationship. No reason to change it now.

"To what do we owe the honor of a visit?" Jack asked. "You weren't scheduled back here for a couple of weeks."

Gabe shot Nick a look. "Coward."

"Figured it was your deal, not mine." Nick had enough on his plate without electing to tell Jack about an injured horse that had cost a small fortune.

Gabe sighed as he walked to the back of the trailer. "Point taken. Jack, I bought a mare." He slipped the bolt on the trailer door. "Before I get her out, I want to remind everybody that Grandpa Archie used to say this ranch was where everyone got a last chance at happiness."

Jack sighed. "What's wrong with her, Gabe? Because with a buildup like that, I'm sure something is."

"She foundered, and the owner was ready to ship her off to the auction. She would have ended up at the slaughterhouse, Jack."

"So I hope you got her for a song."

"More like an album."

Hands on hips, Jack glared at him. "I thought we agreed no expenditures without checking with me."

"I had no time to check! Besides, you would have said no, but I figured if you saw her, you'd—"

"Gabe, you're supposed to *ask*, dammit!" Jack's eyes turned stormy.

"Would you have said yes?"

"No!"

"Well, there you go."

"I don't know why I even bother trying to keep some semblance of order around this place. Well, here's the deal. You take care of her."

Gabe drew in a breath. "But Nick is the—"

"Nick has other duties. You're the nursemaid, Gabe."

"But I'm entered in several—"

"Guess you'll have to drop out." Jack turned on his heel and stomped off in the direction of the house.

Gabe watched him go. "Can he do that? Can he order me to stay here with the mare?"

"Probably not," Nick said, "but if you leave he could sell her."

"I can't believe he'd do that."

"The old Jack wouldn't have," Emmett said. "But we're dealing with a different guy these days. If you want to keep that mare, I think you'd better hang around."

Gabe looked desperate. "But my being out there is good for the Last Chance! I help sell horses!"

"I know." Emmett rubbed the back of his neck. "But those entry fees are mounting up. Even with prize money, it's an expense, and I heard Jack questioning it the other day."

Gabe muttered a swear word.

"Give it a day or so," Emmett said. "Let's get those horses out and stabled. Nick can check out your mare. Then we'll have a beer and you can tell us all about your adventures. I'm betting Jack will show up down at the barn and have a beer with us."

Nick should have taken Emmett's bet, because an hour and a beer later, Jack hadn't shown up. They had rounded up extra chairs, but one of them remained empty.

Emmett polished off his beer and stood. "I'm sure you boys have some catching up to do." He sent a telling glance in Nick's direction. "I have a few chores to finish up before dark. Good to have you back, Gabe."

"Thanks," he said. "Let's hope it's a temporary visit."

"Let's hope." Emmett didn't sound convinced. "Well, see you both in the morning."

After he left, Gabe leaned forward. "That was damned obvious. Clearly, there's something he wants you to tell me. What gives? Is it Jack? Because he's starting to bug the hell out of me."

"It's not Jack."

"Mom? Mom's okay, right?"

"Mom's fine." Nick searched for a way to lead into the subject, but couldn't find one. "Night before last I went through that old trunk of Dad's."

Gabe's attention sharpened. "Yeah?"

"And I found…I found a document that said…" He paused and blew out a breath. "Gabe, a woman named Nicole O'Leary is my biological mother. Not Sarah."

"What?"

"Jack confirmed it. So did Emmett."

"No way." Gabe got up and started pacing. "It's not true. How could that be true? Somebody would have told us!"

"Not if Dad wanted it kept quiet." As Gabe listened in stony silence, Nick laid out the story, or as much as he knew of it.

"That's bullshit, Nick. Dad should have told you! I can't believe he kept it to himself, that he let you go on thinking…" He stared at Nick. "It doesn't change anything as far as I'm concerned. You're still as much my brother as you ever were. Just so you know."

"Thanks." Nick smiled at him. "I feel the same."

"This is incredible." Gabe took off his Stetson and wiped his forehead with his sleeve. Then he glanced up at Nick. "What about Mom? Have you talked to her?"

Nick shook his head. "I saw her last night, but we were having fun at the Spirits and Spurs. I couldn't see the percentage in ruining her evening by telling her I knew."

"Are you going to tell her?"

"Yeah. Secrets suck. I think we should get everything out in the open. But she's in town with Grandma Judy, and I need to tell her face-to-face."

Gabe shook his head.

"What?"

"You think the best plan is to hit her with it while she's looking right at you? I would have *loved* to hear this on the phone, so I had time to get my head around it before I saw you."

"You would?"

"Absolutely. So would Mom, I'll bet." Gabe nudged his hat back with his thumb. "Here's my idea. Call Mom and tell her that you know about this Nicole lady, and now I know. Tell her you love her and you want all of us to get together at Spirits and Spurs tonight for dinner so we can talk about stuff."

"You think Grandma Judy's up for that?"

"I know she is. I called Mom to tell her I was coming home, and she asked if we could all go out. I guess she had a great time dancing with you last night and now Grandma Judy is determined to make it over there even if she has to use her walker."

"I still don't think the phone is the right way to break this kind of news."

"Nick, the telephone is a wonderful invention, especially for information of a sensitive nature. Take it from your little brother, people don't like to be ambushed, which is what it feels like when someone drops a bomb on you in person."

"Did you feel ambushed?"

"A little, but I had that incoming missile warning from Emmett. Call her, Nick." Gabe pulled his phone out of his jeans pocket. "Do it now. I'll be your moral support. She's my third speed dial number."

"Who's your second?"

"You."

Nick hadn't known that, and he was gratified to be placed so highly. "Got a woman on speed dial?"

"Don't I wish. And that reminds me. Mom said you were hanging out with somebody named Dominique last night. But I don't want to hear about her until after you call Mom."

Nick obediently punched the speed dial for his mother's phone, and she answered immediately.

"Gabe? You're home?"

"Yes, he is, but this is Nick, using his phone to ask if you and Grandmother Judy can come to dinner at Spirits and Spurs tonight."

"What time?"

"Six?"

"Great. Will Dominique be coming? I liked her so much."

"No, she won't be able to make it."

"That's too bad. Maybe another time. So, can I talk to Gabe?"

"In a second." Nick took a deep breath. Dominique's voice reminding him of Sarah's love echoed in his head. This would be okay. "Mom, I know about Nicole O'Leary."

Dead silence.

Or maybe it wouldn't be okay. "Mom? You there?"

"Yes. I'm collecting myself. How did you find out?"

"Going through Dad's old trunk."

His mother groaned. "I should have gone through it weeks ago. This is my fault. I'm so—"

"Mom, it's fine. I'm fine. I'm glad I know. At first I was upset that nobody told me, but I'm not upset anymore." And that was also thanks to Dominique, who'd helped him understand that Sarah had acted out of love, both for him and for his dad.

"Nick, I don't know what to say. Except that I love you."

"I love you, too, Mom."

"And no matter what, I'll always be your mother. I'm just sorry you found out on your own instead of from me or your dad."

"That's pretty much what Gabe said." He winked at his brother. "Here he is." Nick handed the phone over and stood up to stretch the muscles he'd unconsciously tightened during the phone call.

The suspense was over. Dominique had left, all the significant people in his life had been informed that the long-kept secret was out, and life could get back to normal. Normal and boring. Without Dominique.

The future looked bleak indeed.

17

As Nick dressed for the evening, Pam called on his cell. Or at least that was the readout. For one wild moment he imagined that Dominique hadn't left, and she was using Pam's cell phone because…because…

When he answered, heart pounding, and heard Pam's voice, he cursed himself for a fool. Still, he couldn't stop himself from asking about Dominique. "Did she get off okay?"

"She's on her way back to Indianapolis."

His heart ached. "Good. That's really good. It's the best for her, the best for me."

"I suppose it is. Listen, she forgot to get a release form signed so she can use those pictures she took of you. I offered to get that done. Should I drop the forms by?"

"That's okay. Gabe and I are going right by your place in just a little bit. We're meeting my mom and Grandma Judy for dinner. Hey, would you like to come along?" Nick realized Pam was another person he should tell about his recent discovery. She'd be hurt if she found out from someone else.

"Thanks for the invite, but I have some things to take care of here. So Gabe's home?"

"Yep. For now, anyway." Gabe's belief in the advantages of delivering startling news by telephone ran through Nick's mind.

"Then I'll see you in a few minutes."

"Uh, Pam? There's something I should probably tell you, rather than have you hear it from someone else. The other night I was going through my dad's old trunk and found this document. Seems that before my dad met Sarah, he had an affair with somebody named Nicole O'Leary."

Pam drew in a sharp breath.

"Is something wrong?"

"It's just that I haven't heard anybody say that name in a long time. It… I'm surprised it still affects me so much."

Nick frowned. "What do you mean? You couldn't have known her. You've only been here about five years."

"I knew her very well, Nick, maybe better than anybody. Nicole was my sister."

"Your *sister?*" Feeling suddenly light-headed, Nick sat on the edge of the bed.

"I knew about her wishes, and after she died I kept track of what was going on at the Last Chance. As soon as I was financially able, I bought this house and turned it into a B and B so I could be close to you. I never had kids, and so…you're my only family."

"You're…my aunt." Despite saying the words, Nick couldn't absorb the concept. It seemed too fantastical.

"Yes, I'm your aunt, and when you're ready, I'll tell you everything I can remember about your mother."

"Whew." Nick closed his eyes. "I'm having trouble taking this in."

"I'm sure."

"Does my mom—I mean, Sarah—does she know about this?"

"No, nobody knows. I was prepared never to tell you, but now that you've found out about Nicole, there's no point in keeping the secret. And you can certainly call Sarah your mom. She has been your mom, and I'm not the least bothered by you calling her that. My sister gave you life, but Sarah gave you a home. Even if my sister had lived, she couldn't have done that. It wasn't in her nature."

Nick swallowed. "Um, look, I know you said you were busy, but are you sure you can't come to dinner? You've always been like family, and now…well, you are family."

"I don't know, Nick. I'm the sister of a woman who might not be your mother's favorite person."

After the revelations of the past couple of days, Nick had a new appreciation for his mother's strength of character. "She'll take it fine. After all, she ended up with my dad."

"And she also ended up with you, and I've seen how much she cares about you. Good point. All right, I'll come. But I'll leave the telling up to you."

"And I'll take that assignment, but I have to admit that all these secrets have been a royal pain in the ass. From now on I hope everyone can be up front about stuff. I've had it with secrets."

PAM PICKED DOMINIQUE UP at the airport the afternoon of the exhibit, which was being held in the evening, complete with champagne and hors d'oeuvres. Dominique had timed her arrival late on purpose, knowing if she came in any earlier, she'd have to fight the urge to go out to the Last Chance to see Nick.

"I still say you should have told him about this," Pam said as she drove the Jeep around to the back entrance of the gallery. "You should have heard him raving on that night about secrets, and how he was so done with them."

"I can imagine, after you dropped your bombshell. I'm glad it all turned out okay."

Pam glowed with happiness. "More than okay. I can acknowledge my nephew and give him the photo albums I've saved for thirty years. Sarah's been great about it, which helps. Everyone's adjusted to the new status quo, but Nick is death on the subject of secrets. You need to tell him you're here."

"I don't dare, Pam. If this doesn't go well…"

"What if it does? You look fabulous, by the way. That yellow dress looks like a ray of sunshine."

"Or an elongated egg yolk. After I bought it I wondered if it was too yellow."

"It's perfect with your coloring. You'll stand out, which is what Stuart has in mind." She gazed at Dominique. "You could still call Nick."

Dominique shrank from the potential hurt. "If I call him now, and he comes for the exhibit and nobody shows up, then this plan is DOA. We'd have to do the goodbye thing all over again."

"Look, I've told you about his belated inheritance

from his grandparents, which has been earning interest ever since they died. Do you think he wouldn't love to use that to set you up in your own gallery?"

Dominique shivered in horror. "There's a recipe for disaster. He shells out the money and I fail. Or he shells out the money and I succeed, but we discover we aren't compatible, after all. I don't care if he's King Midas himself, I won't take money from him to further my career."

"All right, but I'm telling you, he'll hate missing this. It's a huge moment in your life, and you're cutting him out of it. He deserves to make the decision whether to risk coming to Jackson and watching how this turns out. Give him the option, Dominique. Put an end to the secrets."

Dominique reached for her door handle. "Let's go in."

Pam sighed in defeat. "All right. I tried."

Stuart ushered them in the back door, and he was beaming. "You're going to love what I've done with the photographs, Dominique. The samples I sent by e-mail don't do them justice."

Dominique took his hand in both of hers. "I know you're taking a risk with an unknown photographer, and I'm so appreciative, Stuart. No matter what response we get tonight, I'm—"

"Are you serious?" Stuart squeezed her hands and then drew her forward into the gallery. "The excitement has been building ever since I leaked one shot to my steady customers, and it wasn't even the primo picture I love so much. Take a look. People will eat this up."

Stunned, Dominique found herself in a wonderland of her own making. She'd always dreamed of a one-woman show, but she'd never imagined what the subject matter would be. Yet here it was, her instinctive choices matted and framed, hanging from movable walls and mounted on easels. Somehow, without fully understanding what she was doing, she'd captured the cowboy fantasy she'd come to Wyoming to find.

Yes, it was mostly embodied in Nick Chance, but Stuart had interwoven his image with shots of stall doors, bridles hanging from pegs, saddles thrown over a sawhorse, Sundance and Butch lying beside the barn. The impact of all those framed pictures nearly brought her to tears. It was a dream—*her* dream—come true.

"Do you approve?" Stuart gazed at her in gleeful anticipation.

She turned to him. "If I knew you better, I'd hug you."

"Go right ahead."

So she hugged him, short though he was, and just tried to make sure his face didn't get buried in her cleavage. Her dress was sleeveless and summery, with a V-neck that was daring for her. When she'd bought it, she'd wondered if Nick would ever see her wearing it.

And as she wandered around the gallery in a trance, pinching herself to make sure she was actually awake, she knew what she had to do. This show wouldn't have been possible without Nick. Pam was right—he deserved to be here.

Even if he could witness her failure. Despite Stuart's assurances, Dominique knew that the public could be fickle. But she'd already acted extremely cowardly, not letting Nick know what she was doing.

Shamefacedly, she walked over to Pam. "I need to call Nick."

"I'm *so* glad to hear you say that."

"But I don't have his number."

Without a word, Pam reached into her purse, pulled out her phone and hit a speed dial number. Then she handed the phone to Dominique.

Her hand shook as she waited to see if he would answer. Instead she got his voice mail. She took a deep breath. "Nick, this is Dominique. I'm in Jackson at the White Feather Gallery, where they're exhibiting my work in a special show tonight. I'm so, so sorry I didn't tell you earlier. I was afraid the show would be a flop and then I'd be no closer to gaining a foothold here than I was before. But whether it's a flop or a hit, you deserve to be here. It's...it's your show, too. I should have invited you in the beginning. Please come. And don't blame Pam for keeping this secret. I told her to." Ending the call, Dominique handed the phone back.

"So." Pam gazed at her.

"It's up to him, now."

NICK FOUND THE MESSAGE at the end of a long day. Gabe had stayed on to guarantee that his mare would survive, and Nick had worked hard toward the same goal. The mare, named Doozie, was holding her own, but Nick was exhausted, both from taking care of Doozie and dealing with Gabe's frustration at being forced to abandon the competition he loved.

But his exhaustion vanished when he saw who had called. He'd never expected to hear from Dominique again. Had she reconsidered? Was she still in Indiana? Or at the airport in Jackson? Heart pounding and throat dry, he listened to her message.

After hearing it, he found his first instinct was to throw the phone across the room. She hadn't trusted him. She hadn't trusted him enough to let him be part of her plans, and that hurt. Secrets, damned secrets. She'd made Pam a part of another one.

He tried to summon the willpower to ignore the message, but knew he wouldn't be able to keep away from her. She was in Jackson, and in a very short time he could be there, see her again, breathe in her spicy perfume. But what was he potentially doing to himself?

Unsure what he would say or do when he arrived, he showered, dressed in jeans and a comfortable shirt, crammed his Stetson on his head and hopped in his truck. On the way to Jackson he called Gabe to let him know what was happening.

"You watch yourself, bro," Gabe said. "From all you've said, I'm not sure this chick is worthy of you."

"I'll keep that in mind, Gabe." He ended the call and tried to think rationally about this situation. She'd left him saying she wouldn't give up her stable business to chase some potential relationship with him. But at some point she'd made a contact in the gallery.

What did that mean? If she was looking for a way for them to spend time together, couldn't she have told him about it? The more Nick thought about it, the madder he got.

People in his life had a bad habit of thinking they knew what was best for him and he didn't need to be part of the decision-making process. He wasn't about to take that from Dominique. If they were going to have a future they had to start off on the right foot, which meant they'd talk to each other about everything. No secrets.

He had trouble finding a parking place because the area near the White Feather Gallery was mobbed. Gradually, he realized the mob had to do with the gallery. He finally found a space and had to walk a couple of blocks.

Getting in the door wasn't an easy feat, either. People were standing around on the sidewalk outside, champagne flutes in hand. He caught snatches of conversation—*fresh new approach, captured a cowboy's soul, the romantic image of cowboys personified.*

He didn't realize the personal nature of those comments until he caught sight of the first framed picture and recognized himself. Dear God, no wonder she'd said it was his show, too. Belatedly, he remembered the release he'd signed, but at the time he'd thought she'd be displaying the photos in Indianapolis. He'd never expected to see them hanging in his backyard.

A woman with an upswept hairdo and a champagne glass dangling between her fingers approached him. "You look *exactly* like the guy in the pictures! Is it you?"

"No, ma'am, it's not me."

"Are you sure?" She peered closer. "Your nose is exactly like his. And your shoulders, and your—"

"You know how it is, ma'am. All cowboys look alike."

"I know what you mean, but still, I would swear it's you."

"It's not. Now, if you'll excuse me, I'm looking for somebody."

"Yeah, me, too." The woman winked. "I'm looking for that cowboy. Yum."

He finally saw Dominique on the far side of the gallery, talking to more champagne-drinking folks. Before he could make his way over there, Pam intercepted him.

"Hi, there."

"Dammit, Pam, you knew about this."

"Aunt Pam to you."

"Aunt Pam." He still hadn't taught himself to say that, although he wanted to. He loved the idea that Pam was his aunt, although right now he was pissed as hell at her. "How could you keep this a secret from me? You know how I feel about secrets."

"I promised not to tell you. And at the time I promised, I didn't know you'd found that document my sister had drawn up. I didn't know secrets would become your personal sore spot."

Nick glanced around and lowered his voice. "On top of that, most of the pictures are of me."

"Why do you think I had you sign that release?"

"So she could put the pictures up in Indianapolis."

"You could have asked me what she planned to do with them."

"And you could have told me she was in negotiations with a gallery in Jackson." Nick blew out a breath. "Is this how things are going to go with Dominique and me from now on? She makes a bunch of plans, which I find out long after the fact?"

Pam looked at him with obvious amusement.

"What's so funny?"

"You. You're thrilled that she's trying to establish herself here, and you're even thrilled that she's doing it with pictures of you. The only problem is that she didn't let you know in advance. Am I right?"

He rolled his eyes. From the moment she'd met him five years ago, Pam had been able to figure out what he was thinking. Now he wondered if that was because he had certain things in common with his birth mother.

"Nicole always hated being the last one to know," Pam said with a telling smile. "She loved surprising people, but she wasn't big on being surprised."

Nick sighed. "Okay. What now?"

"As you can see, traffic's good. I don't know what the cash register says, though. People might have come for the free champagne and hors d'oeuvres, and not to whip out that credit card."

"I'd like to talk to Dominique, and I'd like to do it someplace private, if that's even possible."

"I'll see what I can arrange. But if I set this up, don't keep her long, and don't smear her lipstick."

"You sound like her agent. Whose side are you on, anyway?"

Pam winked at him. "I'm on both sides. You two belong together, and I'd love to see that happen." She started to walk away.

Something Emmett had said echoed in Nick's head, and he caught Pam's arm. "Did you send Dominique over to the ranch on purpose, because you thought she and I would hit it off?"

Her eyes twinkled, but she didn't answer.

That was enough answer for Nick. "For God's sake, Pam."

"Don't worry." She patted his arm. "It'll turn out fine."

Moments later he glimpsed her guiding Dominique toward the back of the gallery. Pam glanced in his direction and motioned for him to follow her. He did, and was soon face-to-face with a startled Dominique in a small room that smelled of sawdust and was filled with framing supplies.

"Don't be long," Pam said as she closed the door.

"You came." Dominique's cheeks were flushed. "I was afraid I'd blown it by not telling you sooner."

"About that. We need to have an understanding."

"We do?"

"Yes." He couldn't resist touching her, but the minute he took hold of her bare arms, he forgot what he'd been planning to say. All he could do was stare into those big brown eyes and wonder if he could kiss her without smearing her lipstick.

"What sort of understanding, Nick?"

He struggled to regain his original thought. "That two people who love each other don't keep secrets."

Her breath hitched. "You love me?"

"Isn't it obvious? I can't sleep, can't eat, can't go more than five minutes without thinking of you. When I got your message I wanted to be furious with you for not telling me about the exhibit, but I…Dominique, I love you so much."

She moaned softly. "I love you, too. But I wanted to wait until I saw whether this show was a success, and financially, I—"

"I know that's important to you, and I don't want to undermine your independence, but could we make a commitment that we're going to be together, whatever happens?"

She looked at him for a long, long time. "Yes."

"How indelible is that lipstick?"

"Not very."

"Do you have more somewhere?"

"Yes."

"Then come here, you." He pulled her in tight and kissed that sweet, sweet mouth. He was as careful as he knew how to be, but she was so delicious, and he hadn't kissed her in so long.... When he finally made himself pull back, her lipstick was a mess. "You'll have to fix that."

"It's okay." Her smile lit up the small room. "You are so worth it, Nick Chance."

* * * * *

One Chance Man has found his match.
Come back next month to see if Gabe can
leave his horses long enough to find love, too.
Watch for Ambushed!, *available wherever*
Mills & Boon® books are sold.

THE DRIFTER &
TAKE ME IF YOU DARE
(2-IN-1 ANTHOLOGY)

BY KATE HOFFMANN &
CANDACE HAVENS

The Drifter

Charlie Templeton is a wanderer, an adventurer.
But one thing scares him: the chance that he's
permanently lost the woman he loved, the
woman he left. He's going back to Eve...

Take Me If You Dare

Mariska Stonegate's new man is secretly a CIA agent
on the run. And he'll do just about anything to stay alive, including
seducing Mariska one hot, steamy night at a time!

AMBUSHED!
BY VICKI LEWIS THOMPSON

Gabe Chance is blown away by the feisty redhead who unexpectedly
lands right in his bed and, soon enough, his heart! He realises that
Morgan's everything he wants, but she may be attracted by his
ranch...

SURPRISE ME...
BY ISABEL SHARPE

Seduced by his fantasy woman. She's overlooked his intellect and
dodgy haircut. He's totally in love; until he realises *she thought she'd
climbed into bed with his bad-boy brother*!

On sale from 18th February 2011
Don't miss out!

One night with a hot-blooded male!

18th February 2011

18th March 2011

15th April 2011

20th May 2011

Discover Pure Reading Pleasure with

Visit the Mills & Boon website for all the latest in romance

🌹 **Buy** all the latest releases, backlist and eBooks

🌹 **Find out** more about our authors and their books

🌹 **Join** our community and chat to authors and other readers

🌹 **Free** online reads from your favourite authors

🌹 **Win** with our fantastic online competitions

🌹 **Sign** up for our free monthly eNewsletter

🌹 **Tell us** what you think by signing up to our reader panel

🌹 **Rate** and review books with our star system

www.millsandboon.co.uk

 Follow us at twitter.com/millsandboonuk

 Become a fan at facebook.com/romancehq

2 FREE BOOKS
AND A SURPRISE GIFT

We would like to take this opportunity to thank you for reading this Mills & Boon® book by offering you the chance to take TWO more specially selected titles from the Blaze® series absolutely FREE! We're also making this offer to introduce you to the benefits of the Mills & Boon® Book Club™—

- **FREE home delivery**
- **FREE gifts and competitions**
- **FREE monthly Newsletter**
- **Exclusive Mills & Boon Book Club offers**
- **Books available before they're in the shops**

Accepting these FREE books and gift places you under no obligation to buy, you may cancel at any time, even after receiving your free books. Simply complete your details below and return the entire page to the address below. You don't even need a stamp!

YES Please send me 2 free Blaze books and a surprise gift. I understand that unless you hear from me, I will receive 3 superb new books every month, including a 2-in-1 book priced at £5.30 and two single books priced at £3.30 each, postage and packing free. I am under no obligation to purchase any books and may cancel my subscription at any time. The free books and gift will be mine to keep in any case.

Ms/Mrs/Miss/Mr_____ Initials _____

Surname _____

Address _____

_____

_____ Postcode _____

E-mail _____

Send this whole page to: Mills & Boon Book Club, Free Book Offer, FREEPOST NAT 10298, Richmond, TW9 1BR

Offer valid in UK only and is not available to current Mills & Boon Book Club subscribers to this series. Overseas and Eire please write for details.. We reserve the right to refuse an application and applicants must be aged 18 years or over. Only one application per household. Terms and prices subject to change without notice. Offer expires 30th April 2011. As a result of this application, you may receive offers from Harlequin Mills & Boon and other carefully selected companies. If you would prefer not to share in this opportunity please write to The Data Manager, PO Box 676, Richmond, TW9 1WU.

Mills & Boon® is a registered trademark owned by Harlequin Mills & Boon Limited.
Blaze® is being used as a registered trademark owned by Harlequin Mills & Boon Limited.
The Mills & Boon® Book Club™ is being used as a trademark.